DYING DAY

The buggy kept on coming. When it was opposite the point where McCoy had entered the woods, it stopped. He heard a voice.

"Spur McCoy, you stupid bastard, you better start thinking about dying, 'cause that's what you're going to be doing before this day is over. Christ, but I've waited a long time for this."

As soon as the man stopped talking, a shotgun boomed and Spur jerked his head back behind the big oak, as half-a-dozen big slugs hit the tree and the brush around him. Double-ought buck! He knew how well it killed, but he had never been on the receiving end before.

Also in the *Spur* Series:
SPUR #1: ROCKY MOUNTAIN VAMP
SPUR #2: CATHOUSE KITTEN
SPUR #3: INDIAN MAID

SPUR #4

SAN FRANCISCO STRUMPET

DIRK FLETCHER

LEISURE BOOKS NEW YORK CITY

A LEISURE BOOK®

August 2003

Published by

Dorchester Publishing Co., Inc.
276 Fifth Avenue
New York, NY 10001

ISBN 0-8439-2117-X

The name "Leisure Books" and the stylized "L" with design are
trademarks of Dorchester Publishing Co., Inc.

Printed in the United States of America.

SAN FRANCISCO STRUMPET

CHAPTER ONE

(Oleomargarine, the common man's butter, was patented by H.W. Bradley in Binghamton, N.Y. in the year 1871. Ulysses S. Grant was President of the United States. The National Rifle Association was organized in New York City. The first of many Chinese Tongs in San Francisco, Kwong Dock Tong, was organized a year earlier and was growing in strength. Cement was patented by D. O. Saylor in Allentown, New York. Wild West outlaw Ben Thompson surfaced in Abilene, Kansas, the first cow town, and began a lifelong feud with Abilene Town Marshall Wild Bill Hickok. In October 1871 the great Chicago fire destroyed Chicago with an estimated loss of more than one hundred and ninety-six million dollars.)

Spur McCoy adjusted the white tie he wore with his formal evening coat and relaxed. It had been a month of holidays since he had been in a formal suit — not since he had worked in Washington, D.C. He sipped a cup of slightly spiked punch and watched the ladies in their beautiful long gowns and the men in white tie wearing a version of what San Francisco's social set considered formal wear.

And it was society. This was the official celebration of the opening of the San Francisco Opera Society's 1871 season. It was a gala evening. The performance of *Don Giovanni* was fair, Spur decided, but the lady who just danced past him was remarkable.

He watched her over his punch cup. Maybe five feet five, taller than most women, and the proud, determined way she held herself when dancing piqued his interest. She was a brunette, with hair to her waist in a silky black waterfall, and he thought she had brown eyes in the moments he saw her face. A round, pretty countenance, with wide set eyes, and a small nose over a pouting mouth.

The soft pink gown cinched delightfully at her waist, and the top showed a generous amount of soft white breasts and a dark line of cleavage.

Yes, he would have to dance with this one.

Spur was in San Francisco on business. He was a Secret Service agent of the United States Government, with St. Louis as his base, and he had the entire western half of the nation as his territory. Which meant he was seldom in St. Louis. The Secret Service was still the only federal policing agency that could cross state lines, and as such it was called upon to handle a wide range of problems.

His current assignment was simple: find and stop a major counterfeiting ring in San Francisco that specialized in minting double gold eagles, the gold twenty dollar piece that was still the only solid medium of exchange considered as actual hard money by many cantankerous Westerners.

The pair danced back toward him in the large Pacific Ballroom, and Spur moved quickly through the dancers and tapped the young man on the shoulder. He turned.

"May I cut in?" Spur asked.

He saw a glint of surprise and pleasure dart across the woman's face. Twenty-five, he judged.

"Oh, damn, not another one. Katherine, you are simply much, much too popular tonight."

The man stopped talking, shrugged, bowed gently and walked away.

"May I?" Spur asked again.

She put one hand on his shoulder and held her other out to him.

"Of course. And a man with manners in San Francisco! Really, I am going to have something to tell everyone!"

He accepted her hand and danced her around the room.

"I know we haven't been introduced, but when I saw you I couldn't stop myself from cutting in. If I may say so, Katherine, you are the most beautiful lady I have seen in a century and a half."

She laughed, a small tinkling sound that sounded

exactly right for her. She leaned back in his arms to get a clearer look at him, and smiled, one dimple showing, her eyes crinkling slightly as she nodded.

"Yes, I like you. Now, so we can be formally introduced, I am Katherine Sanford, of *the* Sanfords. He's my father although sometimes he is loath to admit it."

"Delighted to meet you, Miss Sanford. I am Spur McCoy, but I am not a cowboy. I come from New York City by way of Washington, D.C. and St. Louis."

"A New Yorker! I knew you had to be someone special. And you dance beautifully. Could you hold me just a bit closer so I can follow you better? Yes, that is ever so nice. I love it."

They circled the ballroom, and Spur was getting used to the heady scent of her hair and the interesting perfume she was wearing when someone tapped him on the shoulder. He stopped and stepped back. Spur saw the girl shaking her head at the man behind him, but Spur already was thanking her for the short but provocative dance, then the young man whisked her away into the rest of the dancers.

Spur went back to the punch bowl, then to the person in the room he knew best, J. Anderson Dumbarton II, one of the biggest bankers in San Francisco, a man who had a knowledge of his city and his thumb on its pulse as well as anyone.

Dumbarton was a tall man who could look eye to eye with McCoy at six feet-two inches. He had considerably more girth as well as financial reserves and resources. He waved a welcome to Spur as he walked up.

"McCoy! Glad you could come. How did you enjoy our opera? We'll all proud of the organization we have here. Our Opera Society seems to fall apart every few years, but we've got it in high gear now. And I see you picked the prettiest girl in the place to dance with already. You always did have a good eye for the ladies."

"Jay, good to see you. I found your note and the tickets on my dresser when I checked in this morning. Thanks, I enjoyed the music. How is the banking business going?"

The financier frowned. "Fine, except for that little problem I wired you about. It isn't out of hand yet, but I'd hate to think what would happen if the story gets out. We weather bad publicity about the paper certificates every year or two, but the double eagle is the standard."

"That's why I'm here, Jay. I'll be past your firm in the morning to check over those items you have to show me. You have caught twenty of them so far?"

"Twenty-two now."

"That's bad. But to more pleasant topics. What can you tell me about Katherine Sanford?"

"As much as you want to know. Daughter of Amos Sanford, the Sanford Emporium, the biggest and best mercantile in town. You can buy anything from a diamond necklace to a steam engine at Sanford's. He's a whiz at sales and promotion, probably the

11

best man on advertising goods we have in town. Daughter is just like him, bright, quick, even graduated from college. She and her father don't get on the best, both a hell of a lot alike, on the stubborn side."

"And she's not married?"

"Nope, she must be twenty-five or twenty-six now and that's one of the problems. Old man wants her married off and out of his hair."

"Thanks. And I'll be in about nine tomorrow."

"Fine, fine, now don't stand here, go out there and cut in on her again."

Spur did. She smiled.

"What took you so long?"

"Checking up on you. You are a Sanford."

"Yes, now hold me close before I scream."

He did. Halfway around the floor there was a set of french windows leading to a patio. He headed for them, and she smiled as he opened one and motioned for her to go through. Outside he closed it, saw no one else there and took her in his arms and kissed her lips tenderly.

"Yes," she said when their lips parted. "That was nice. Mr. McCoy, do you believe in impulses?"

"Usually, do you?"

"Always. I have a tremendously strong impulse right now to kiss you back." She stretched up on tiptoe and held his face and kissed his lips hard. When her lips came from his her eyes opened and she nodded. "Oh, good lord yes!" she said softly, took his hand and led him across the patio to another set of french windows which opened inside to a hallway, and down it on the right, she opened a door and went through it quickly.

A lamp burned low on a dresser. It was a waiting room, with several chairs, a couch and two mirrors.

She reached up and kissed him again, then turned to the door and threw a small bolt.

"Spur McCoy, would you think it terribly bold of me if I asked you to kiss me again?"

He shook his head, took her in his arms and kissed her. As he did he felt her push against him, from her ankles right up to her hips and then her breasts pressed hard on his body. His mouth softened to hers and his tongue flicked out, brushed her lips and suddenly they were open.

McCoy gave a little moan of pleasure and thrust his tongue deep inside her mouth, finding her tongue and dueling with it, chasing it, struggling to capture it again. Then he withdrew and waited and slowly her tongue darted in and out of his mouth, then came in firmly in command, probing, pushing, exploring.

When at last their lips parted, she sighed.

"Now, that, Mr. McCoy, was a real kiss." She looked up at him a moment, smiled, then took his hand and put it over the bareness of her upper breasts.

"I'm hoping that you have some impulses right now that you would like to follow, Mr. McCoy."

She reached her hand down and rubbed it over the growing bulge at his crotch. Katherine smiled, and with one deft movement pulled her dress off one shoulder, and then the other, letting the fabric slip

13

slowly down until it revealed her breasts.

Spur's hands caught them, his fingers massaging them as if they were rare gems, exploring her heavy nipples, brushing them until they heated and rose and filled with hot blood to stand even taller. He could feel her breasts throbbing.

Her hand had opened the buttons on his fly and wormed inside, grasping his erection.

"Darling! Darling!" she breathed softly.

Spur bent and kissed her pulsating breast and she whimpered. He kissed the other one.

"Yes, yes, sweetheart!" she crooned.

Spur bent lower and nuzzled her big orbs, kissing around and around, then winding up at her nipple. He kissed it firmly and bit the brown bud until she yelped in joy. His mouth continued to work until he was sucking on her nipple, pulling half the big tit into his mouth as Katherine gasped and moaned and leaned back against the door.

Her hands were busy as they worked his stiff pole from his fly. She cried out in success when he came out and she sank to her knees in front of him, staring at his penis.

"So wonderful, marvelous, so beautiful!" She kissed the stem and saw him jump. She kissed him again, and then worked toward the purple headed tip.

It was Spur's turn to moan in delight as her soft lips closed around him and she licked and sucked his rod. It had been a week for Spur and he wasn't sure how long he could take this kind of specialized treatment. He looked at the couch, then lifted her up.

He kissed her lips, looked deep into her eyes and found her nodding.

"Yes, yes, and quickly, I am ready, darling, I am so ready I am almost undone."

He started for the couch, but she pulled him back, leaning against the door and lifted her skirts. She wore no other garments. She pulled her skirts to her breasts, spread her legs and leaned against the door.

"Darling, kiss me," she said. Spur dropped to his knees and parted the fragrant, dark hair to see her pink nether lips and he kissed them, then again as she crooned above him. He found the magic node and he twanged it again and again with his tongue until she shrieked in ecstasy, her hips driving against his face as she trembled and shook and cried out. The tremors boiled through her slender body and her hips pumped a dozen times against him.

Somewhere in the process she lost her hold on her skirts and they billowed around Spur, but he held one cheek with each hand and kept massaging her clit and driving his curved tongue deep into her wet and eager pussy.

That set off another series of climaxes and she held his head through the cloth fast to her crotch while she vibrated through another long shattering series of climaxes. At last they trailed off and she sighed, then giggled and lifted her skirts and petticoats, and used them to wipe off his mouth and his face. Holding her skirts she pushed her legs wider apart.

"Your turn, darling."

Spur bent his knees, moved toward her and she directed him until a moment later he plunged into her wet heartland and drove upward until his pubic bones ground against hers. Katherine let out a long wail of delight. She screeched with delight as he began to surge upward into her, retreating and then claiming her vagina as he own, again and again.

"Darling that is so beautiful!" She said. "Darling you make me feel like a real woman. That is fantastic! You are so fine, so fine!"

He felt the pressure growing, slowed and stopped, then he bent low until he could pull her breast into his mouth and suck it. As he did she climaxed again and it set him off on another pounding driving set of thrusts upward into her.

Somewhere deep in his system the small valve opened and the trigger pulled, the hammer dropped, and he could feel the primer charge go off, igniting the main powder supply and ramming his load upward through the tubes, along the highway of no return, until he cried out in joy and rapture. He jetted his load into her grasping and throbbing vagina.

As he finished he wanted to slump to the floor. But she held him tightly against her body, keeping him upright, nailing his body inside of hers.

It was five minutes before she sighed, and let go of his back.

"Just beautiful, darling Spur. I've never fucked anybody against a wall this way. It was tremendous."

Spur grinned at her vocabulary, sucked in air trying to get his breath and his strength back. It was true what they said about Samson, only it wasn't cutting his hair that made him weak.

She hurried to the dresser, found a towel and turned to minister to herself. Then she lowered her skirts, and walked toward him with her breasts bare.

"One more kiss?" she asked. "It will be the last time you ever see them or ever touch them. I won't even dance with you again so don't try. I like it this way. Always something different, someone new."

He bent and kissed each breast, licked her nipples and felt them rising again. She turned away.

"No!"

"Katherine, I will see you again. I will make love to you again, only the next time on my terms, in my bed, and with lots of time." He bit each nipple until she shuddered and then moved up and kissed her mouth. When he broke away from her he saw her self-confidence decaying. He kissed her once again and made sure that his clothes were arranged properly. He slid the bolt open and left the room as she worked at getting her breasts covered and her dress properly adjusted over her shoulders.

Spur left the gala, and headed for his room at the San Franciscan Hotel. It was just about two A.M. He wanted a good night's sleep before his work day tomorrow.

Spur McCoy was a big man, standing six feet two

inches and hitting the scales at two hundred pounds. He had sandy red hair, a full red moustache and sandy mutton chop sideburns. He was an excellent horseman, a crack shot with derringer, six-gun or rifle and was in fine physical condition. He could fight with a gun, knife, his fists or a four foot staff.

Not many people knew that Spur McCoy was a United States Secret Service Agent. The service was established by an act of Congress in 1865 with William P. Wood as its first director.

Spur came to the service by a round-about way. He was born and educated in New York City, went to Harvard and graduated in the class of 1858 at twenty-four years of age. His father was a well known merchant and trader in New York, and after two years with his father's import business, Spur joined the war time army with a commission as a second lieutenant and advanced to a captain's rank before Lee surrendered. After two years in the army, Spur went to Washington as an aide to Senator Arthur B. Walton, a long-time family friend from New York. In 1865, soon after the act was passed, Charles Spur McCoy won an appointment as one of the first U.S. Secret Service Agents.

Since the Secret Service was the only federal law enforcement agency at the time, it handled a wide range of problems. Many were far removed from the group's original task of preventing currency counterfeiting.

Spur had spent six months in Washington's Secret Service office, then was transferred to head the base in St. Louis where he handled all problems west of the Mississippi river. He was chosen from ten men because he was the only one who could ride a horse well and because he had won the service marksmanship contest. Wood figured the man in the west would need both skills.

CHAPTER TWO

Spur McCoy had walked only half a block from the Pacific Ballroom when he sensed that someone was following him. He had turned toward the San Franciscan Hotel, which took him down a side street with fewer lights in the buildings. He had no weapon with him, with the exception of a hideout derringer strapped to his ankle. As soon as he turned the corner, he ran hard for fifty feet to an alley mouth and stepped into the darkness.

McCoy pulled the derringer out, checked the loads by feel, then held it ready for his trackers.

Two of them came around the corner quickly, looked down the street and stopped. McCoy stepped into the street sure that they could not see him in the gloom, but they could hear his boots against the bricked-in sidewalk. He strode confidently away from them, listening behind him. Two sets of footfalls continued to follow.

Spur slowed, reversed his direction and walked toward the pair. It was some time before they realized what had happened, and when Spur was almost upon them, he ran forward attacking. McCoy slammed into the smaller man spinning him sideways into the street where he fell. The second man caught an angry left lead fist into the gut which doubled him over. The small man got to his feet and ran.

Spur patted the man down, found no weapon and spun him around and slammed him against a store front. He took too long to recover and when he started to lift his head he came up with flying knuckles in front of him. Spur slammed his fist down on the back of the attacker's neck, dropping him to the sidewalk on his face.

Spur followed him down, planted his knee in the middle of the man's back and put all his weight on it. He grabbed the ambusher's head and turned it where Spur could see it.

"Talk, you son of a bitch before you die. Why the hell were you trying to follow me?"

"Wasn't, wasn't following nobody."

"Hell you wasn't. You want me to find a policeman and have you thrown in jail?"

"No, no!"

"Then talk, fast."

"Don't know who he was. This gent gave us a dollar each to find out where you was staying."

"Who was he?"

"Didn't know him. Some swell in a fancy suit like yours."

"How were you to tell him my residence?"

"Write it down and take it to this address."

McCoy took the slip of paper and read the numbers in the faint light. It was a downtown address, probably some business. McCoy slid the paper in his pocket and took out a small, thin one dollar gold piece. He gave it to the man.

"Thanks, friend. There is your dollar. Now you don't need to take care of the delivery, I'll handle it myself. I expect a much bigger payoff when I find out who this gentleman was."

The next morning Spur was up and dressed promptly at 6:30, went downstairs to the dining room where he ordered a breakfast of steak with scrambled eggs, a stack of hot cakes and hot syrup. He finished with coffee and read the *Examiner*. There seemed to be no burning problems in the world, and, most important, there was no story about counterfeit gold double eagles being circulated in San Francisco.

He had been in San Francisco many times during the past few years, and never ceased to be surprised by the vitality, the cosmopolitan atmosphere of the former village now all grown up. Ships from dozens of nations were anchored in the harbor. Many different races were represented in the people walking the streets.

Spur walked a few blocks to the Dumbarton-

Pacific Bank and went inside. It was the most impressive bank building in town and fairly shouted that it was four-square and solid, firm and safe for your money.

On the second floor, behind two secretaries, Spur was ushered into the private office of J. Anderson Dumbarton, founder and majority stockholder of the bank. He looked a little worse for his late night out.

"Just a touch of the scurvy this morning, McCoy. Sit down. I have those items we discussed."

Spur looked at them critically. There was little counterfeiting done on gold coins since it was technically so difficult. It involved a foundry, usually plating and always a big stamping press to strike off the coins themselves. When they did find counterfeited coins, many of them were of excellent quality and workmanship.

Some of these were good, some not. One had been sawed in half. The gold on the outside was real, but it was paper thin and had been put on the blanks by simple gold plating. There were places on the finished coins where the sharp edges would lose their gold plating and in other spots it had chipped off. These were the obvious forgeries and easy to spot. Others were harder.

"An even dozen in there. Some are real, some ringers. Can you pick them out?"

Spur found two of the real double eagles, but was not sure about two more.

"Two out of three isn't bad, McCoy. Actually the two you are suspicious of are genuine, just well used.

The other bad coin is so good we weren't sure until we nicked it and turned up the copper, zinc and lead base metal."

"Any more clues who might be passing them since your wire?"

"None, not of any value. We did trace back one of the coins we took in deposit, but it could have been picked up anywhere."

"Is the person reliable?"

"Totally, but she can't remember where that particular coin might have been given to her. She wrote a draft for cash at another bank, but surely they wouldn't have passed it, unless it was a new teller who hadn't proper training. You know the lady, by the way, she is Katherine Sanford."

"Curious," Spur said. "Seemingly little motive for her to be involved in something like this. Must have been duped somewhere. What about the San Francisco police?"

"I haven't alerted them. It would be in the papers at once. This seemed the best way. We don't need a run on the banks for anything as ridiculous as this."

"Right. Could I borrow one of these for comparison?"

"Take any of the bad ones you like. I'd suggest the perfect one for a tough look."

Spur took the paper from his pocket with an address on it. "Oh, I have an errand and I can't remember this street, Olivera, do you know where it is?"

"Olivera, yes, it's down in the edge of Mexican Village. It's a tough neighborhood. Makes the

Barbary Coast look like a church picnic. Be careful."

"My Spanish is passable."

"Is this some kind of a lead?"

"That's what I'm going to find out."

They parted and Spur caught a hack in front of the bank and asked how far it was to Olivera Street.

The driver flicked his reins on the bay's back and scowled.

"You don't want to go there."

"Why not?"

"You're not Mexican. They eat you alive."

"Why?"

"You're a *gringo*. That's Juan Pico's street. It's only one block long. He owns every building on it, and every cutthroat on the sidewalks."

"Let's just drive through."

"No, anywhere else."

"Let's drive past the end of the street."

The one-horse-rig driver thought about it. "For a dollar, and we go fast."

It looked like any of the other streets in the area. A lot of wide Mexican straw hats, women in colorful clothes, shops, markets, stores. So why would someone from Olivera Street try to follow him last night?

He pondered it as the hack drove him back to his hotel. It gave him a moment to think over his leads in this case. The only hard facts he had were the twelve counterfeit coins. From Washington he had received the names and last known addresses of two convicted coin counterfeiters in San Francisco. He had little hope for either. Counterfeiting paper bills was so much simpler these days with the good printing presses available, that the talented men had moved from coins to paper long ago.

At the hotel there were three messages. One was from a Mrs. Mildred Engleton. She said she was membership chairman of the San Francisco Opera Society and wanted to talk to him about becoming a sustaining member. He remembered her from the dance, a large, pretty woman draped in diamonds who was quick to tell him she was a widow. She was about forty.

The second note was unsigned. It said: "I know you are with the Secret Service, others do also. Be on your guard."

The third note was from Juan Pico. "My Dear Mr. McCoy. I must see you as soon as possible. Come to Olivera street and give this note in Spanish to anyone. You will receive every courtesy and be brought to my office at once." McCoy read the Spanish words at the bottom of the paper. He didn't understand all of them but in essence it said that the bearer was a friend and was to be taken to Juan Pico's office at once.

Ten minutes later Spur was back at the entrance to Olivera Street. The cab driver let him off and hurried away. Spur had walked only ten feet down the street before a large Mexican with a scar on his cheek stepped into his path and muttered in Spanish. Spur held out the paper and the man scanned the bottom of it quickly, returned it to Spur and motioned with his hand to follow.

They entered a new three-story brick building

near the center of the block. Spur noted that it was the same address as the note he'd taken from the pair who tried to follow him. The building was well made and decorated with Mexican murals and framed paintings. The lobby was spacious with two desks and luxurious furniture. Up an open staircase he could see offices with glass walls. They went up the steps and then on to the third floor where the scarred Mexican knocked on a wide beautifully hand-carved oak door. It opened a moment later and a well dressed woman glanced at him, then smiled.

"Yes, you would be Mr. McCoy. Won't you come in. Mr. Pico has been hoping that you would come. Right this way."

She led him through an outer office furnished and decorated with an understated elegance that surprised Spur. It looked like a senator's outer office in Washington. The small dark girl knocked once, then opened the door and walked inside. Holding the door for Spur she motioned him inside.

The office was luxurious with thick carpet, original oil paintings on the paneled walls. Two large windows looked down on Olivera Street. The whole office was professionally decorated with a decided macho theme.

Spur took this all in with a glance, then turned to the man sitting behind a massive cherrywood desk. He stood and held out his hand. Juan Pico was tall with soft brown Mexican skin, dark eyes and a lot of black hair which he combed straight back. He wore spectacles which he now held in one hand.

"Mr. McCoy. I have been trying to get in touch with you. It is good that you came so quickly."

Spur took the hand and met the firmness with equal force.

"Thank you, Mr. Pico. I have heard a lot about you in a short time."

"Do not believe all that you hear, Mr. McCoy. I am here only to help my people, to see that they are treated fairly, and that they can live a good life." He waved Spur to a softly upholstered chair at the side of the desk. Now to business."

Spur had not heard the door close behind him, but assumed it had. Now he sat and looked at Juan Pico. Before he could say anything he felt cold steel pressed against his neck and the ominous sound of a six-gun cocking. Spur did not move, he only looked up at Pico.

"Yes, Mr. McCoy, a gun at your head ready to kill you. I promised you every courtesy in my note, I said nothing about killing you. Tell me, Mr. McCoy, Secret Service Agent for the United States Government, how does it feel, knowing that you are about to die?"

CHAPTER THREE

Spur felt the cold gunmetal at his neck and chuckled deep in his throat. "No, no, Señor Pico. I simply can't believe what you say and what the pistol suggests. It is not reasonable, it is not rational, it would not be good for your people, and mostly because you obviously are a cultured man, a person of taste, breeding and education. But the main reason why you did not invite me here to kill me is because it would be of no value whatsoever to your people. And that, Señor Pico, is your purpose in life, your reason for being, your goal, your mission."

The slight sneer on Juan Pico's face faded and was replaced by a grudging smile. As his smile broadened the pressure of the gun muzzle eased and then stopped as the weapon was removed.

"Si, Señor McCoy. They told me you were no ordinary man, no run of the mill civil servant. I had to be sure what kind of a man I was dealing with. Now I know from my own experience." He stood and reached out his hand again. "Now I take your hand as a friend. Come, I want to show you something."

He moved to a case along a wall with a glass top. Inside there were gold double eagles. He opened the case and motioned for Spur to examine them.

"Yes, counterfeit, all of them I would imagine, or they would not be here."

"True. So far we have found a hundred and twelve. That represents two thousand, two hundred and forty dollars. Which would have been a tremendous loss to my people. The average shop owner in the street below makes a net profit of between eight to ten dollars a month, with his whole family working ten to twelve hours a day. He cannot afford a twenty dollar loss, even once a month. The bank has *retained* ten of these coins which had been deposited by some of the larger businesses. I have made good on these others to my people."

Juan Pico paused and watched Spur closely. "I understand that the prime responsibility of the United States Secret Service is to control and stop all counterfeiting."

"That used to be our only task. Now our duties have far outreached that and we handle any interstate felony problems."

"But counterfeiting is still a major work?"

"Yes, Señor Pico. That is why I am here, to stop this particular counterfeiting." He took the perfect counterfeit from his pocket and tossed it to Pico.

"The work is excellent. Only the thinness of the gold plating gives it away."

Pico examined it, found the gouge where the base metal showed through and frowned. "It is good work. I don't think I would have caught this one." His black eyes snapped. "So what can we do about it?"

"Have your people seen anyone passing them? Could it be a Mexican? Not many *gringos* shop on your street."

"That is the bad part. We have seen no *gringos* passing the coins. Most are new like this one, and only through use do they grow tired and we catch them."

They went back to the desk and sat down. Spur rubbed his hand over his face for a moment in thought. "Señor, would you do me a favor?"

"Of course, that is why I invited you here."

"Ask each of your people to nick every twenty dollar gold piece they take in with a knife, gouging it to see if the gold is plating or real. Then they should get a description of any person trying to pass the bad coin. A caution. There may be many of these counterfeits out there passing as real. Innocents must be using the coins without knowing it. But we may be able to establish some pattern of passing and perhaps spot one or two persons."

"That will be done within the hour."

"Don Pico, have you lived in San Francisco for many years?"

"Since my birth, Mr. McCoy."

"Good, you and your people must know this city

as few others could. It is a complicated process this counterfeiting of gold coins. Certain unusual equipment must be available. Could you discover for me where in the area such coins could be produced? There would need to be some basic foundry and metal working and plating equipment, as well as a heavy metal forming press or stamping press, the kind needed to strike the coins from the plated base metal."

"Yes, good. We can have that information within twenty-four hours. There will be no *siesta* or *mañana* here. We will find all the places where such work can be done. They should be both in the same plant?"

"Yes, that seems logical."

The same small woman who had let him into the office appeared with a tray holding coffee and some confection. They were a foot long and dusted with powdered sugar.

"Coffee?" Pico asked. Spur nodded. "You must try this sweet we have. We call it *churro*, something like a long donut."

Spur sipped the coffee, then took a bite of the *churro*. It was like a light, delicious donut, tasteful and sweetened with powdered sugar. Before he realized it he had eaten a whole one.

Pico nodded. "Yes, there are few who do not love our *churros*." He became more serious. "Mr. McCoy, we need your help. We do not often ask for outside assistance. Our Mexican community likes to think it is self-sufficient. We are not, of course. We do not even have our own bank. But we are growing.

Olivera Street has a bad name among the Americans. You will hear that it is filled with cutthroats and thieves. That is not true. We are hard working men and women protecting ourselves, and trying to make a living."

He motioned to the door and two men came in. They were well dressed in white shirts and neckties and dark trousers. They were young and well groomed. They listened attentively to Juan Pico and the instructions he gave them in Spanish. A moment later they were gone.

"Come, let me show you Olivera Street, introduce you to my people, and you will see how gregarious, outgoing and loving they are. Anytime you wish to walk Olivera Street and buy a *churro* or other goods, you may do so with total freedom and absolute safety. Already I am spreading the word that the tall *gringo* in the soft gray cowboy hat is our friend. Come."

They toured the street, which turned out to be an area seven blocks long and three blocks wide. It was filled with shops and businesses of all types, and everywhere Don Pico went he was treated with utmost respect, and McCoy sensed a deep love and appreciation of what he was doing for them. Spur bought a sack of *churros* and a softly delicate lace *mantilla*.

Don Pico chuckled when they left the shop. "My friend McCoy, you are a true *gringo*, you do not bargain. You paid the first price you were asked. The *mantilla* could have been purchased for half what you paid."

It was Spur's turn to smile. "Don Pico, I have haggled with the best that Tijuana, Mexicali, Nogales and Ciudad Juarez have to offer. But here, with the people of Don Pico, I gladly pay what is asked as one small way of helping."

Don Pico blinked tears from his eyes and grasped Spur by his shoulders and kissed both his cheeks in a familiar manly embrace of the greatest respect.

"Señor McCoy, you are one of us, you are *amigo*. We thank you."

Spur had the *mantilla* wrapped at a shop and addressed it to Katherine Sanford, and asked Don Pico if he could hire a messenger to deliver it. A boy of twelve hurried up at Pico's call and Spur gave him a quarter to deliver the package. The boy's eyes grew large and he asked if it all was for him. Spur nodded and the youth smiled broadly as he ran down the street.

An hour later Spur finished his tour of the *barrio,* and caught a hack back to his hotel. He munched *churros* on the way and gave one to the driver who said he had seen them but never tasted them. He was happily surprised.

At his hotel Spur wrote two short letters, one to Jay Anderson Dumbarton at his bank telling of the one hundred and twelve counterfeit coins Don Pico had found, suggesting that the situation was much worse than they first assumed. "There could be hundreds more coins out there circulating undetected. This could cause a serious economic problem, even business failure for some small businesses. Suggest holding all coins for eventual reimbursement by some means."

His note to Katherine Sanford was short. "Miss Sanford: The lace was so beautiful that I thought of you, and could not leave the shop until I had it sent to you. Hope to see you again soon." He signed it McCoy.

At the desk downstairs he got envelopes, addressed the notes and had the desk clerk find someone to deliver them for a quarter each.

Back in his room, Spur thought for a moment about Katherine Sanford. She was the most vigorous and responsive woman he had ever known. Every little touch and caress seemed to explode her sexuality. He would see her again, he was positive. He wondered what she would be like over a bottle of wine and some cheese and a big hotel bed with a lock on the door and all night to make love. It was only a dream, but a delightful one.

CHAPTER FOUR

For the first time that day, Spur McCoy thought about his cover. He had come to San Francisco as a representative of his own art wholesale house in New York on a buying trip. He would have to spend a respectable amount of time looking at art. He sized up the list of four galleries and individual artists whom he was supposed to contact in the city. He picked out one with the most impressive name: San Francisco Artists.

The address was only a short distance away, so he changed jackets. He wore a soft blue with his dark blue trousers and a flashy vest of blues and greens over his white shirt and tie. He decided that he looked artistic enough.

San Francisco Artists was off the main streets on the ground floor with a dozen good oil paintings exhibited in the window. He went inside, heard the bell ring and a small man with a large belly, rimless spectacles and a smudged white painter's smock came through a connecting door.

"Yes, may I help you?"

"McCoy is the name, McCoy Galleries in New York City."

His pleasant expression sweetened to delight.

"Mr. McCoy! Pardon my appearance. A commission I'm rushing for a dear lady on the hill. Look around a moment while I change and I'll show you everything we have. Just a minute."

Spur knew enough about art to bluff his way through. He favored naturalism, without a lot of shifting around of the subjects. And in portraits, the mole better show or he was not pleased. He noticed several paintings that were good. At the end of the display room one painting was positioned where it caught the morning light and was highlighted with reflecting mirrors from two angles. It was a seascape, a rocky area and a cliff with a glittering sunset. Close in the foreground there were two seagulls. It was an outstanding painting. He guessed it would bring over a thousand dollars at a New York auction.

The little man came back, his hair slicked down and wearing a suit coat to match his pants. His eyes shone with anticipation.

"Well, Mr. McCoy. The art colony here must be thrilled with your visit. We have some outstanding artists in town and we all pull together. Here at my gallery we have over twenty professional artists represented. All local, and all excellent."

"I'm sure they are, Mr. . . ."

"Excuse me, the name is Locklaw, Ira Locklaw."

"Mr. Locklaw, I'm looking for specifics. One type painting I need is marine oils. Do you have any good ocean scenes, beaches, rocks, cliffs, the mighty Pacific in a storm, that sort of thing?"

They spent an hour sorting through paintings, and Spur quickly selected half a dozen he was interested in. The painting on the wall had been discussed first. The artist wanted five hundred dollars for it but Locklaw said he would take less from a New York gallery just to get his work shown and owned there.

"Would you like a drink, Mr. McCoy? I could go with a spot of Irish whiskey about now with just a brace of branch water."

Spur nodded, studying the painting of the ocean on the wall again. It was an excellent job and easily worth the thousand dollars he'd originally estimated.

The whiskey came cut with only a splash of water and Spur worked on it slowly.

"I do have one other item to show you, Mr. McCoy. It's called *Triplets*. Three interesting female figures. It's in the back studio. Would you care to see it?"

Spur waved his drink and followed the pauchy little man. It was in the back studio which had excellent northern exposure and a skylight. The canvas was a large horizontal, three by five feet. There were three woman on it, all nude and in various provocative poses. The background had been completed and the figures half filled-in.

The little man was wringing his hands.

"Of course it's only started. I have all the detail work to do, but what do you think of the concept? I'm calling it three wood nymphs . . . as in nymph-omaniacs."

"Your basic composition doesn't excite me, Mr. Locklaw. Not that it's wrong or bad, but it just doesn't move me. This is obviously for a select audience. Whoever buys it will want it to be sexually explicit, to arouse him, to excite, to stimulate. Have you considered mixing a man in with the three women?"

Locklaw stood for a moment frozen in thought then he smiled. "Yes, yes! I think the patron who's interested would be enthusiastic about such an addition. Yes! Would you like to see the models themselves? They are still here since they were sitting for me." He didn't wait for Spur's response, but waved his hand and there was motion behind a screen Spur had seen to the right.

Three young women came out wearing white cover-up robes. One was a striking Chinese girl with long black hair. She had a pouting face that could not be called pretty, but the gown was wrapped around what Spur had seen on the canvas, a voluptuous body. The second girl was a blond with her hair cut short. She was small, slender with a quizzical smile. On canvas she appeared to be fuller bodied than in real life.

The third girl was a huge Spanish girl. She was

older than the other two, perhaps twenty-two. Her jet black hair was cut short, and the robe had slipped open in front. She was about five feet two and must have weighed more than two hundred and fifty pounds.

"Ladies, ladies! This is no time for modesty. You are models, your bodies are your fortunes." Spur saw that Locklaw was rubbing a bulge behind his fly. "Come, come, ladies, let's get to work. Pose on the mattresses, now!"

They went to three single blue mattress pads on the floor and each took off her robe characteristically, Spur decided. The tall Chinese shrugged it off her shoulders letting her large, heavily nippled breasts surge out, then flipped the white robe away as if it were a trifle. She lay in her position on the mattress with her slender legs spread, one straight, one knee bent, and leaning up on one elbow, her other arm draped across her knee, her breasts bouncing slightly with her movements.

The small blonde turned half around as she slid the robe off, then in a teasing move walked to the pad and turned so that Spur could see her front as she assumed her pose. She stood with her legs spread, her blonde crotch hair glistening, her legs bent and her hands lifting her breasts which were small and delicate with light pink nipples and aeolas.

The heavy Mexican girl knelt on the pad, her huge breasts sagging almost to the floor as she presented her chubby ass to the artist. She looked over her shoulder with what Spur decided was her version of a coy expression.

Locklaw was openly rubbing his erection now through his pants.

"Mr. McCoy, that is what I call arousing. God, doesn't it get your pecker up?"

The artist dropped to his knees on the floor, pulled open his fly and jerked out his hard penis. "Oh, God, you kids are just beautiful, so sexy, so damn sexy!"

It was a signal. The girls dropped their poses. Two of them simply sat down and waited. The small blonde moved toward Spur. She rubbed against him and then began unbuttoning his vest.

"Damn, but I'd like to see you naked as I am."

"You are a pretty girl."

"And sexy? Do you want to fuck me?"

"Of course."

"Then get your pants off."

"They watch?" Spur asked amused.

"The girls won't be able to stand it for long. It was my turn first. Old Ira there will play with himself for a half hour then want to work again and put us in those asshole poses."

She had his vest unbuttoned and half his shirt. She pushed her hands inside touching his warm skin.

"Oh, nice! I like a man with chest hair. I go wild playing with it." She pulled his hand up to her breast.

"You like tits? Start out with these and work up to the Chink and the greaser. They got cow tits."

Spur laughed and fondled her breasts. "Can you feel that? Do you respond at all?"

"Shit, not to that little feel. I'll get going about the third time. I ain't no fucking virgin, you know." She had his pants unbuttoned and his underwear down and pulled out his still limp prick.

"Hey, fuckers, look! A man with some staying power. Tits don't get him hard!"

The three girls cheered. The others came over and helped pull off Spur's pants. Then they carried him to the biggest mattress and flopped down beside his prostrate form.

"Come on, Tiny Tits, you was first," the Mexican girl said.

The blonde yelped and rolled on top of Spur, then knelt over him and worked on his hardening staff. She gave a little cry of success and positioned herself over his hips and holding his penis upright, she stabbed it into her vagina.

"Oh, lordy, I ain't lost the fucking touch!" she shouted. "I still got the way in the hay, I smooch in the kooch, I'm a hell in the bell, and I fuck like a duck."

Spur hardly moved. She lifted herself off him and plunged back down and soon achieved a familiar rhythm. Forgetting that he was on the bottom, Spur responded as he always did with a jolting, hip-thrusting climax that pitched the blonde three feet in the air and brought squeals of admiration from the naked girls.

As soon as the blonde was impaled, the other girls lay down beside Spur. The fat girl held his hand to her huge breasts, urging him to play with them. The Chinese girl leaned close to him, tongued his ear and assured him that she was *not* cut sideways as the myth warned. She plunged his hand between her legs and squeezed it, then let him find his own way into her heartland.

Spur looked at Locklaw. He was on his knees, his right hand pumping his surprisingly long penis in the traditional male masturbating pose. Sweat beaded his forehead but still he pumped and pumped, his eyes fastened securely on the four naked bodies on the mattresses, anticipation showing on his face.

Over him the blonde was screaming, wailing, pumping at Spur harder than ever as she climaxed again and again.

Suddenly she was gone. The big Mexican girl had shoved her to one side, breaking their connection.

A large brown face loomed over Spur.

"Honey-fuck, now you gonna see something, a real Mexican ten dollar piece of ass. You know how *good* that is? Shit, you don' know." She bent and put a piece of elastic three times around the base of his penis and laughed.

"Yeah, now we got that big prick captured. He ain't gonna droop on Carlotta, tell you that for sure." She got up on her hands and knees and pushed her big bottom toward him. "Hey, man, you got it up, get it in. You the big toro and I'm the little heifer in the pasture. Plant it in me, Big Cock. Sock it right in my old pussy!"

Spur was getting into the swing of it. He got on his knees and powered forward, heard a shriek as he entered and then a long squeal and a moan.

"That's too high, you're in my fucking asshole."

"Enjoy it while you can," Spur said, reached around her and grabbed a big tit with each hand and pumped into her, slapping with each stroke against her fat buttocks.

Carlotta bellowed and moaned, screeching so loud it caught Locklaw's attention. He climaxed, jolting his load into his hand, but kept right on pumping for seconds.

Carlotta kept up a steady stream of moans and chatter.

"You sexy prick, you can't get me pregnant in there. What the fuck I have to show you how to do everything? Bet you don't even piss straight. Damn like to have you for a month. I'd get your ass straightened out. Get some good chilli beans and peppers into your gut and clean out your asshole. Yeah, and you could ream mine out every night. Oh, shit-fuck but that is wild. You a mean fucker, man, a mean fucker."

Spur worked it up a long time, then knew the rubber band was stopping him. He pulled out of her, slid off the elastic band and jolted back into her upper slot and climaxed almost at once, slamming her forward onto her fat belly on the mattress, bringing a wail of torment and ecstasy from Carlotta who gave one last shuddering climax and went to sleep without moving.

He pulled out of her and turned to find the Chinese girl with her large, shapely breasts kneeling in front of him. She had a wash basin, warm water and soap and she washed off Spur's genitals tenderly, yet thoroughly. She smiled.

"Mr. McCoy. We save best for last. I born in Hong Kong. Do not know American ways. Only Chinese way, all right?"

Spur nodded. He wasn't doing much to find the counterfeiters, but hell, he had to maintain his cover. Too many people in town already knew that he was Secret Service. That could get him killed. A good cover was worth its weight in gold.

"Little darling," Spur said. "I don't think there's anything you could do that wouldn't be all right with me."

She smiled. "Name, LoLing." She bowed.

"Shit, here we go again," Carlotta said.

LoLing ignored the jibe and began a soft little chanting song in Chinese. It fascinated Spur who had no idea what she was saying, nor did he understand the strange musical sound, but still he was caught up.

She finished the song and bowed again, then took his hands and placed them gently on her breasts. "Play," she said.

Spur felt himself suddenly shoved to one side. Locklaw knelt there glaring at Spur.

"Not this one. LoLing is mine. All mine. You fuck around with them other two sluts, but nobody touches LoLing but me!"

Spur watched him for a moment, looked at the inviting, lush young body of the Chinese girl, her heavily nippled, large breasts and her slender waist and perfect legs.

"Yes, Locklaw. Yes, I can understand that. I

understand." He stood and found his clothes and let the small blonde girl help him put them on. She buttoned every button and pulled on his half boots. Then she kissed his fly.

"When you coming back? You wanna come to my place? Not much but it's got a quiet bed." She laughed. "Sure, you think I'm a slut just because I like to fuck. Hell, men like to fuck, why can't a woman like to pump it up the way men do? No goddamn reason. Men just afraid of us. You wanna come over to my place right now, stay a week or so? Fuck this job. He can do the rest of it from memory, he's been in me enough in the last two months so he won't never forget me. How about it?"

It took Spur a half hour to get untangled from the girl with the short blonde hair and back to the street. Locklaw was still entwined with the gorgeous LoLing, and Spur didn't blame him a bit.

McCoy checked his watch as he stood outside the gallery. He would have time enough to get to the U.S. Mint and find out more about how they made gold coins as well as some of the major problems that counterfeiters confront. He found a hack and was soon talking with the professionals in the field of minting coins. He would learn as much as he could, as quickly as he could and then see what Juan Pico had turned up. There was a good chance that Juan's men could find out what he needed to know and do it much faster than Spur. He needed all the help he could muster.

CHAPTER FIVE

Katherine Sanford sat in her room in the Sanford
Mansion high on the hill and studied her reflection
in the mirror. Yes, she was pretty, and her figure
was good enough to trap almost any man she wanted
whether he was married or not.

She studied the eyes, brown, with tiny flecks of
emerald green. Yes, but were they excited? Were the
eyes ready for something new? Someone new? A new
thrill? Damn right they were!

And it would happen today. Katherine had awakened that morning cheerful and happy, realizing
that she had enjoyed a new experience the previous
night. Good Lord, she had been fucked standing up
against the door twenty yards from the Opera
Society's gala dance! Now that was worthwhile! And
the man, this Spur McCoy, had certainly put his

spurs into her. Usually she forgot the man an hour later, but there was something about this one, this cowboy who was sleek and slick and intelligent and surprise of surprises, had manners. That held her interest.

Yes, she was ready.

She went out the side door, walked three blocks down the hill to a cross street where a row of small houses stood. They were quaint and poor and she always wore a cover-up bonnet when she came. Now she slipped in the side door of one of them, relocked it after her and went to the back bedroom. There she tore off her clothes, the skirts and petticoats, the wrapper, the fluffy drawers. She wore only a cut-off pair of drawers and a thick, tight chemise that bound her breasts close to her chest.

Quickly she put on a shirt too big for her that bagged at the chest covering her breasts, hiding them. She stuffed the shirt tail into a pair of breeches that were also cut slightly large for her figure, concealing her womanly hips. Her hair had been braided and pinned securely on top of her head before she came. Now she pinned on a hat with a dozen pins so it couldn't fall off, and put on knee-high boots.

She looked at the effect in the mirror. A pair of thick rimmed spectacles with plain glass completed the disguise. Her own mother wouldn't know her from three feet away. She smeared dirt smudges on her cheeks, and wiped off the rouge she had put on last night. With a mask added to her disguise there would be no way anyone could identify her.

Kate went out the rear door into the alley, saw that no one was there and walked quickly down the street to a livery and rented a gentle nag she had used before. So far she hadn't said a word. Her voice could be a problem.

She rode for an hour and left the fringes of houses at the south of San Francisco behind. Less than a mile ahead and only a quarter mile off the main trail down the coast in the direction of a growing community known as Los Angeles, sat a small farm house. She rode to the rear where four more horses stood.

Kate tied her horse to the rail and went in the back door. As she opened it she heard someone say:

"Easy, it's her for sure."

Kate walked into the farm house kitchen slapping a riding crop against a gloved hand. She looked around at the familiar room and at the four men waiting for her.

"Gentlemen. You are all here. Good. Any changes in our plans?"

Foster Burke, who went by the tag of Foss, hunched his shoulders and stood.

"Kate, we got to thinking. Can't see much profit in this one. Twice we hit them before and sure as hell they going to have more guns out this time. Seems like one hell of a big risk when we got a sure thing going tomorrow night."

Burke was the best gun in the group and the tallest at five feet ten. He also had an annoying habit of exaggerating things. It offended Kate but she tried not to let it show. He had been much easier to handle since she had taken him to bed and promised him more later. He had a shock of red hair they always had to keep covered and one missing tooth that showed when he smiled. She guessed he was about forty years old.

"I've told you each time that this is a volunteer operation. Anyone not wishing to go is excused. Of course, you also know it's a little like fishing. You never know who or what you might catch in the stage from Los Angeles North. And as is always the case, I take no share in anything that you find.

"There might be twenty dollars in silver and two pocket watches, or there might be a bank strong box on board with fifty thousand dollars worth of gold in it. The choice is yours."

Kate looked at Tim Hackett, a man five feet tall who was the best metal worker and die man she could find in San Francisco. He was even tempered, about thirty-five and married. He was also an excellent locksmith. Now he pawed one hand back over straggly brown hair to cover the growing bald spot on top and shrugged.

"I like to fish, it's a gamble. Hell, I'm in the game if we get enough players."

The third member of the team was a Klamath half breed raised in Oregon and who had learned English at his white father's knee. He was the best tracker in half of California, and good with horses, with a natural instinct to calm them.

He nodded. "Yes, I'll go."

She looked back at Foss. He shrugged. "Christ the three of you would bungle the whole thing and get somebody killed. I better go along and keep you out of trouble."

Kate smiled. "Then it's unanimous, since Hop Choy always votes with me."

When he heard his name, a huge Chinese looked up from where he sat on the floor. He was six feet eight inches tall and weighed three hundred pounds. But he was all muscle, no flab. He had been neutered as a boy in Canton by a regional War Lord to be a guard for the Lord's women. But the War Lord was defeated and the victor freed all the slaves. Eventually he was captured near the coast and sent to the new world to work on the railroad. Afterward he drifted to San Francisco where Kate saw him, befriended him so she could seduce him, and only after two tries did she realize that he was mute as well as castrated. The War Lord had cut out his tongue. She set him up in her house and supported him, using him in various ways when she could.

Kate smiled. "Well, then, we still have a few minutes. Our original time schedule called for us to leave here at 10:30. It is now fifteen minutes from that hour. We will have ten minutes of dry shooting practice. Burke will direct."

They went in back and Burke again gave them directions in the best way to fire a six-gun, and the best way to hit a target. Burke was a natural teacher, and an excellent shot with any weapon.

Promptly at 10:30 they mounted up and rode out. Each wore a blue handkerchief around the throat ready to be pulled up as a mask. They rode ten miles along the coach road south to a spot where it entered a thick patch of live oak and brush.

Burke positioned them where the roadway made a turn and the rigs would slow. He was the only one with a rifle, a heavy Sharps with a .50 caliber slug and enough stopping power to drop a horse in its tracks.

Hackett, with a shotgun would be front insurance, Burke was at the bend in the road and would stop the rig. Hop Choy was at the back and would let the rig pass him. Kate was on the up trail end near Hackett, and the Breed would be sandwiched between.

Burke had worked out the strategy on the first stage they took two years ago in Nevada, and he had not varied his plan. They all were in position a half hour before the stage was due. Knowing the schedules the coaches maintained, they realized it could be from one to three hours late.

Today they were lucky. A half hour after its due time, they heard the rig coming up the trail. Burke cocked the big Sharps and rested it over a fallen oak tree that hid him and offered him excellent protection in case of a fire fight.

All his people had protection.

Five minutes after they heard the rig they could see it. It swung around the bend and Burke was standing following the lead horse. He head shot it and the animal died in mid-stride going down in the traces. The other five horses tried to bolt ahead but twelve strong reins in the driver's hands pulled them down after dragging the dead animal for less than forty feet.

Burke had positioned himself perfectly. The rig was opposite him. As the harness stopped jangling he called out.

"Guard! Pitch your shotgun and pistols into the trail, then stand up and hold your hands on top of your heads. You too, driver, only tie them reins tight first. If them horses move, you die!"

The orders were carried out.

"Now listen carefully and no one will get hurt. There are ten men around you, you are surrounded." As he finished Burke fired a pistol shot under the coach. The four others fired at the same time.

When the noise died down Burke called out again.

"Everyone inside, get out and sit in the road. Do it now, facing the trees."

Slowly the door opened and two men and two women got out. Then out came a small boy and an elderly woman.

Burke called to the youth. "Boy, use that black hat and gather up everyone's wallet, watches, jewelry. I can see all of you, so no holding back. If you think that hiding a twenty dollar gold piece is worth your life, you are betting your life on it. Do it, son, right now."

It took nearly five minutes for the boy to gather up the money and jewelry the passengers were carrying.

According to the plan Breed had crossed the road below the bend and come back on the off side, worked to the coach and checked the interior. He jabbed with his knife and a cowering man in a black suit erupted from the coach.

"Well, well, a coward, a holdout. Walk straight toward my voice, sir, we'll see what you are trying to hide." The man looked behind him, saw Breed's war-painted face and the ugly knife thrust at him. He walked.

In her position to the rear, Kate saw the man and giggled. She knew him, a pompous ass, one Reginald Compton. She was glad Breed had flushed him and wondered what Burke would do. He had strict instructions that no person was to be harmed in any way.

As Compton vanished into the woods toward Burke, he called out again.

"Now, the strong box up there in the boot. We know where it is, driver. Take your hands down now and toss it to the ground. Then unhitch your lead horse and see if you can move this lopsided buggy around the animal."

Three minutes later the dead horse had been cut free and the coach maneuvered around it.

"Thank you, son, for your help. Now, put the gentleman's hat with the loot in it on top of the strong box, then everyone place beside it any personal weapons you might have and reboard the coach. Your journey will continue shortly."

There was a scream from the woods, and Reginald Compton came running from the trees. He was stark naked, and ran behind the coach. He refused to move until one of the men gave him a coat to cover himself.

"Driver, move it out!" Burke called and fired the rifle again over the heads of the men riding on top. "Get it out of here!"

As the coach rolled along the trail, the men who had been ahead of it fired a shot behind it to keep it moving. Soon it was a dot two miles down the road.

"Let's take a look," Kate called and they all ran into the roadway. Burke looked over the wallets and jewelry.

"Maybe two hundred dollars worth," Burke said.

Hop Choy lifted the strong box and slammed it down on the top of a buried boulder at the side of the roadway. The wooden box split apart and the top flopped open. It contained no big gold shipment.

Kate looked in the envelopes. She smiled.

"Not such a bad day. Two bank envelopes each with five hundred dollars in it!"

Everyone cheered.

"Now, let's get out of here. Everyone take a different route back." Kate was directing. "Burke and I will bring the loot. Remember, all jewelry to be sold must be taken to Los Angeles or Sacramento, someplace well away from San Francisco. Let's get moving."

Burke and Kate rode knee to knee for a mile straight toward the coast after the group split up. She watched him and nodded.

"Burke, I think you deserve a bonus after today's performance. You were excellent. If nobody can see a stage coach bandit, nobody can identify him or his horse. Beautiful!"

She kicked her horse. "I feel like a swim in the surf. Race you to the water!"

They came out at the beach in a deserted stretch of gently sloping sand and crashing Pacific waves. They dismounted and tied their horses to some brush. She stood close to him. "You haven't said yet if you want your bonus."

He reached down to kiss her, but instead she put both her hands on his crotch and rubbed. A few seconds later she smiled.

"Yes, I think he's saying he wants his bonus." She stepped away from him and began pulling off her clothes. There was no one within sight a mile in each direction. She was naked in thirty seconds and Burke stood watching her with mounting excitement.

When she ran for the water he undressed and followed her.

They jumped waves and swam in the cool Pacific as long as they could stand it, then raced to a grassy place and lay in the sun until they were dry. They made love three times before they dressed and rode back to the farmhouse. The men would be happy, they had earned three hundred dollars each. That was as much as a cowboy earned working all year on a ranch!

Kate watched her gang, her team, she called them. She reminded them that they would work the next night. Two of them were assigned to stop at the small house to pick up the gear they needed before gathering at the usual place.

"Three or four more sessions with the press and we should be set for life," Kate said.

"Good," Burke said. "I'm getting the feeling that it's about time for me to be moving again. Hate to overstay my welcome anywhere."

Kate watched them, they were a good crew. She signaled to Breed. He would ride with her back to town. One of these days she would give *him* a bonus. He was the only one she had not favored, but he didn't seem to mind. On the way to the small house she told him he would get a bonus the next night. He stared at her a long time, then nodded, and rode back to the ranch house.

CHAPTER SIX

There was a note in McCoy's key box at the San Francisco Hotel when he returned from his research at the U.S. Mint. It was a message inviting Spur to dinner with Don Pico at a restaurant in the Mexican Village at seven. It also indicated in a guarded way that Pico had some useful information. The note had been sealed, opened and sealed again.

Spur wondered if someone was watching him or if it had been a desk clerk's idle curiosity. To be sure he didn't make himself an easy target, Spur slipped out of the hotel by the side door. He had changed into a lightweight, white summer jacket.

Don Pico was waiting for him at *La Valencia* restaurant, and was working on a frosty, salt-rimmed *margarita*. Spur ordered the same and Don Pico came at once to the point.

"We have found twelve small and large foundries in the area, and four of them contain the large stamping presses you mentioned that were essential to counterfeiting. As you suggested we did this quietly."

"Good. I'll go on a midnight patrol and check them out. Do you have the addresses?"

Don Pico handed Spur a paper with the names and locations neatly printed, including small maps of each to pinpoint the location.

"Thank you, highly efficient."

Don Pico smiled. "Efficient help produces excellent work. I only have highly qualified people around me."

They had not ordered but dinner came. First *tortilla* chips with a spicy dip that set Spur's mouth on fire. He used up two glasses of water. Don Pico smiled and signalled for a milder *salsa*. The appetizer was finished and a series of courses came, each could have been a full meal. Spur ate until he was stuffed, and held up his hands.

"I surrender, Don Pico, everything was delicious. I'll learn to eat that hot *salsa* yet."

The Mexican leader smiled. "Perhaps, Señor McCoy. Now, back to business. May I offer you some assistance? I have two young men who could work closely with you if you wish in any capacity. They both speak excellent English, can use weapons, know the city thoroughly, and have had training in unarmed attack and defense."

Spur shook his head. "Thanks, Don Pico, but I wouldn't know what to do with bodyguards. So far it doesn't look like anything that I can't handle. I'll keep them in mind if I need some quick help and I really appreciate your offer."

"They will be available at any time, day or night. Just send word to me at my office, and say where they should meet you. They will come armed." Don Pico paused. "This is the top task on my schedule, Mr. McCoy. It is vital that we put a quick stop to this dastardly drain on my people. We are struggling, and twenty dollars sometimes looks like a fortune to a small pottery maker. I believe that you understand."

An hour later Spur was back in his room in the hotel. He decided on a good night's sleep before investigating the foundries. He would go to them tomorrow, posing as a small manufacturer of decorative fences and gratings. That way he could inspect the facilities with the help of the owners. It was not only legal, it would be easier.

There were no messages in his key box, so he went up to his third floor room. He walked to the fourth floor, waited a moment and stepped part way into the open stairway going down and waited. No one seemed to have followed him. Good. He went back to room 310 and locked it securely behind him. As an added precaution, he put the key in the lock and turned it half way so it could not be pushed out. Then he wedged a straight backed chair under the door knob. Now he felt safer. It was a five storey building so no one would be climbing up to his window.

He blew out the lamp and lay on the bed. The

weather was still warm, even at night. For a moment he wondered what Katherine Sanford was doing. He laughed remembering the quick, sexy time they had together last night. It had been a total serendipity for him. He was thinking about her luscious body as he drifted off to sleep.

It should not have wakened him. Spur wondered what time it was. He rolled toward the outside of the bed and slid softly to the floor. The bedcovers humped up in the middle of the bed and a bright moon outside beamed a ray of light inside. He saw a shadow at the window and found his six-gun on the chair by the bed and cocked it just as the window shattered and gunshots boomed from outside. Three slugs tore into the covers of the bed where he had been. Before the last shot sounded Spur had snapped off two rounds of his own toward the figure at the window.

Spur heard a cry and then nothing more. He rushed to the broken window and saw a sturdy rope hanging down. He looked through the shattered pane and spotted a figure sliding down the line to the ground thirty feet below. Spur took a quick shot, missed and the figure hit the dirt running and darted behind a buggy in the alley and was gone.

Who in the hell was that? Spur wondered. He must have come down the rope from the roof to the third floor room window. Spur pulled on his pants, then his boots and shirt and went down to the desk where he registered under three different names in three different rooms. He left the registration in 310 under his real name.

Spur pushed his six-gun muzzle under the clerk's chin.

"Son, if *anybody* knows about this, and I mean one other person besides you and me, I'm going to carve your heart out and eat it for lunch! Am I making an impression on your small mind?"

"Yes, sir, Mr. . . . ah, Mr. Green."

"Good. Now remember that. I know you will."

Spur went up the steps to room 310, left his suitcase and took some essentials and slept the rest of the night in room 322. No one bothered him. His new worry was now who out there was trying to turn him into dead?

The next morning, Spur got up at 6:30, dressed in a new lightweight cotton suit and had breakfast. He turned in his 310 room key but kept the other three in his pocket. He found a livery and hired a horse and a rig for a week and made arrangements to bring it back when not in use and at night.

He found the first foundry on the list. It was not large and specialized in small decorative iron pieces and even some jewelry metal work. The big stamping press was seldom used now, and the owner even tried to sell it to Spur. He could see the rig had not been worked for months.

The second foundry was at the far north end of San Francisco, and Spur enjoyed the drive. He was near the ocean for a while, then the street curved back inland and he saw the smokestacks of the foundry. This was a large one, with a great volume of heavy steel work. There were a variety of heavy stamping presses and plenty of capacity for the plating needed for counterfeiting. Spur did not use his prospective customer story here, saw what he could and left. It did not look like a likely prospect for the counterfeiters' use.

The last two spots he checked were closer to the downtown section, along the bay and smaller in size. There was no night work done there the guard on the gate had said. Spur's tour of the second place told him that the equipment would work well.

All that would be needed to operate clandestinely was to bribe a guard or two and use the equipment late at night or early in the morning. He decided that he had better watch both these foundries.

By the time he got back to the hotel it was past lunch time. He wandered to the wharf and ate crab fresh off a boat. A little stand sold a cupful of a tasty seafood sauce along with a dozen crackers for ten cents. He had two of the crab cocktails and a bottle of cold beer. Spur had always wanted to be a fisherman, going to sea every morning, working the poles and nets and coming back at night with the catch. The open sea and the struggle and battle with the elements appealed to him.

When this assignment was over Spur told himself he was going to go fishing on one of the boats. He should be able to find a small boat owner who would take him into the bay fishing, maybe even out to the kelp beds along the coast. Yes! That would be a small pleasure he could look forward to.

Back at his hotel he found a message in his 310

box. He took it up to his room, found that the hotel had reglazed his window with a new pane of glass, and then sat on the bed and read the note.

It was on scented lavender stationery and Spur hoped it came from Katherine. It did not. The paper inside was also lavender. It had been written in a flowing, neat hand. He looked at the second page and saw the signature, Mildred Engleton. He thought back to the gala, yes, Mildred, the membership chairman, a large, pretty woman about forty who quickly told him she was a widow. He read it:

My dear Mr. McCoy. I do hope you don't think me a nuisance, but I would love to talk to you about New York. It has been some time since I lived there, but it would be interesting.

Of course, I will try to talk you into supporting our San Francisco Opera Society as a sustaining member. I have a dozen reasons why you should join.

Would you do me the honor of coming to a small dinner party this evening at seven? I know this is short notice, but it came up quickly and I wanted to be sure to invite you. I will be devastated if you can't come. No reason to reply, just be at the address below at seven and I will be in heaven!

Remember, part of the civic duty of those who have been blessed with more than average wealth is to realize their responsibility to use their money to promote the cultural activities of our city.

I just know that you will come, so I am counting on it. Until seven this evening. . . .

Spur felt trapped. She was playing on his cover story, and the assumption that he was rich, and that he *owed* something to the community. Perhaps he could make an appearance, say he would support the Opera Society, and then beg off pleading an appointment. That sounded reasonable. He did have to maintain his cover for a while yet.

That decided, Spur drove, where he had wanted to go all day, up the hill to the elaborate entrance. A uniformed butler answered the bell. When McCoy said he would like to speak with Katherine, the butler brightened and hurried away.

It was almost ten minutes before Katherine came down the curving marble stairway from the second floor. She wore a soft pink dress that looked so thin it wasn't there, but multiple layers defeated his straining eyes.

Her long black hair was braided, forming twin ropes down her back. She smiled and ran up and kissed his lips quickly, then caught his hand, and led him into a garden greenhouse, off the living room.

"That was so sweet of you to send me the *mantilla*. It is just beautiful. You are an intelligent, cultured, manered, and sexy man. I think I'll marry you for a week." She giggled and led him behind a big fern and kissed him hard, pressing her hips against his until his hot blood began to flow.

"Thanks, but I'm busy this week, so I can't marry

you. However, I would like to take you to the theater tonight. Shakespeare's *A Comedy of Errors* is being played by a traveling troupe. . . ."

She kissed his lips into silence and pushed her breasts hard into his chest. When she leaned back she shook her head.

"Sweetheart, I would love to go tonight, but I can't. Some damn social thing. But why not tomorrow night? Will they still be playing?"

"Yes."

"Then why don't we go then?"

"Fine, I'll be here about 7:30."

She put her arms around him. "Hold me close, sweetheart. I missed you so much. I wanted you in my bed last night so we could make love all night long. Maybe tomorrow?"

He nodded. Her hand worked down to his crotch, and Spur pushed his hand through the folds of the bodice until he could hold her bare, throbbing breast in his hand. She sighed, kissed him one more time and pushed him away.

"Another minute of this and I'll be flat on my back in the orchids spreading my legs," she whispered.

He stepped back. "Yes, Miss Sanford. Then until tomorrow night for the Bard." He turned, walked into the living room where he found the butler ready to open the door to the hallway. There was a twinkle in the man's eye, and Spur figured he had seen the fondling in the greenhouse.

Spur was walking to his rig at the curb when the sound of a pistol shot jolted him back to reality. He

71

dropped to the ground and looked around. He saw a man aiming another shot from around a tree. Spur jumped and ran behind his horse. He worked back and pulled out a six-gun he had hidden in the buggy seat and returned fire hitting the tree. The man's weapon evidently jammed.

Spur ran hard for the tree, firing once more into it. He saw the man look out before he turned and charged down an alley, over a fence and into another yard before vanishing. Spur stopped. The man had been terrified at being shot at. He was running on adrenalin and fear and no one could catch him. McCoy got back in his rig and drove away. No one in the posh neighborhood came out to investigate the gunshots. Either it was common enough or they simply did not feel involved.

Something bothered Spur that he couldn't tie down. The man's face. That was it. He had seemed familiar. McCoy knew he had seen that man before and had dealt with him. The more he thought about it the more convinced he became it had been on an official basis. Where had he arrested the man?

By the time Spur got his rig back to the alley behind the hotel and checked his message box, it was mid-afternoon. He decided to have a bath, and ordered hot water for the third floor bathroom. He enjoyed a sudsy tub until the water cooled. He checked the counterfeit coins in his possession and was ready to leave for his dinner engagement at 6:45. Spur decided to look over the two small foundries for any unusual activity that night. He would leave the dinner party as soon as he could get away. A little support of his cover was all right, but he didn't want to let it monopolize his time.

CHAPTER SEVEN

McCoy parked his rig on a street in the Nob Hill section of San Francisco near the Engleton Mansion. It was two minutes after seven and Spur wondered where all the other buggies were? Perhaps people had been dropped off by drivers and the carriages were parked somewhere else.

He went to the door hoping he wasn't overdressed. Spur was wearing the same basic formal outfit he had worn for the Gala, plus flashier studs and cuff links.

Before he rang the bell, the door opened. Mrs. Engleton greeted him in a floor length gown of sequined gold and wearing a large diamond necklace around her throat which fell into a thrust up cleavage. Her smile was one of delight.

"Mr. McCoy! I am simply overwhelmed that you

have come. It was one of my greatest desires, and here you are. The stars are indeed kind to me tonight. Do you believe in astrology? Well, my dear, you should, it is simply fascinating." She took his arm possessively, her large breast pushing comfortably against him.

"Come in, come in, I want to show you my house. Would you mind? I'm still fascinated with everything that my late husband had built into it for our pleasure. This is the entrance hall, and that funny bathtub is an Egyptian sepulcher, which dates back to the early pre-Christian era. My husband loved Egypt."

The house was a mansion and Mrs. Engleton spent an hour showing him every room, including her bedroom, done in pink satin. She lingered there for quite some time.

Spur kept wondering where the other guests were. They had not yet seen the dining room.

"Mrs. Engleton, this is all remarkable, but where are the other guests?"

She smiled and led him to double walnut doors that opened into a dining room with a table that would seat forty. At the far end next to a large bay window stood a table set for two.

"Dear Boy, I thought I explained that. I said it would be a small dinner party. It's for the two of us, of course. I hope you didn't misunderstand."

McCoy recovered in a second. He smiled. "Then I have you all to myself," he said.

She beamed. "Dear Boy, you do say the sweetest things. Now, let's have a cocktail before dinner."

They sat on a shaded terrace and looked out over the lights of the city. They could trace the bend of the bay and see faint traces of the Pacific ocean far to the west. They sat close together on a couch and her thigh pressed against his through the cloth. She didn't move away. Dinner came a few minutes later.

They went inside and sat at the small table. Their knees touched under it, and she smiled.

"I do so like the small, intimate dinner like this. Then you can really get to know a guest." She sighed. "Spur McCoy, it has been a lonesome ten years for me living here without Wally. He was the most romantic man I have ever known. The patio was his favorite spot. He would take me out there and put down a blanket and seduce me. He didn't have to, but he told me to fight him off a little, he said it made it all the more sweet." She turned. "I hope I'm not embarrassing you. But a relationship is special. Have you been married, Mr. McCoy?"

"No."

"Pity, what a waste! But I bet you have entertained a young lady or two in your bedroom." She laughed. "Yes, I would say a goodly number." She moved and her knee pressed higher on his leg.

Dinner came, a seafood delight. Fresh lobster with melted butter, a dozen clams on the half shell, broiled salmon and the largest, crusty fried shrimp Spur had ever seen.

A small black girl in a maid's uniform complete with little cap served the meal. Her skirt was so short Spur could not avoid seeing the starkly white panties she wore under it.

When she brought the second course she had removed her jacket and the low cut blouse showed more than half of each of her small breasts.

Mrs. Engleton looked at her pointedly. "Celeste, my dear, you do look too warm this evening. Why don't you get cooler?"

"Yes, Ma'am. Right away." Celeste set the tray of desserts on the edge of the table, unbuttoned the blouse and let it drop to the floor. Her chocolate brown breasts had dark, nearly black areolas, and her small nipples were jet black. She wasn't the least concerned with her top nakedness. She served Mrs. Engleton a strawberry tart, and then offered the tray to Spur.

"Take whatever appeals to you, Mr. McCoy," Mrs. Engleton said.

Celeste leaned in toward him, her breasts the closest dessert to Spur. He smiled at her, took a French cheese cake and put it on his plate. As Celeste moved her breast brushed Spur's cheek as she walked away.

"A dear girl, Celeste, but sometimes a little too proud of her dainty figure. I didn't think you would mind my helping satisfy her small fantasy."

Spur grunted a response. He had been pleasantly surprised when the girl was asked to strip, evidently for his amusement. Now he saw the pattern and he had to suppress a chuckle. This society *grand dame* was trying to seduce him, teasing him on with the black breasts and saucy bottom. He wouldn't be surprised if little Celeste came out the next time bare-assed naked.

But there was no reprise. Mrs. Engleton put down her fork and stood.

"Mr. McCoy, I hope you don't mind if I call you that, I've never been a first name person. Please come this way. Oh, I am interested in your participation in our Opera Society, but I understand you will be here only a short time. Pity. I hoped we could count on you for support."

"I really do have a great number of charities . . ."

"Yes, that is what I expected. Don't worry about that. What I have ready for you is much more important. I want you to see my art collection."

They went to the third floor and in a door that opened to a hallway. On each side of the hall were pedestals with African tribal statues and fertility rite objects. Some were obvious, a twelve inch phallus and huge testicles. Others were breasts and variations on a woman's pubic area.

On the last pedestal stood a lifelike woman figure with her naked legs spread and her hands opening her nether lips. The statue came alive. It was Celeste who ran ahead and opened a pair of double doors into a large, high ceilinged room.

"This is my treasure, Mr. McCoy."

Spur looked around in amazement. It was an art gallery. The walls were covered with expensive oil paintings, the floor spotted with statuary, and every art object was pornographic. They were sexually explicit, men and women having intercourse in every imaginable position; homosexual lovers, trios of lovers and one depicted six naked bodies connected in a chain.

"This is my hobby, my love," she said softly.

Spur turned and looked at her. She slowly let down the front of her dress revealing big, firm breasts with the largest nipple he had ever seen. She brushed them with her hands, the diamond necklace extending between them.

"Tonight is for us, Spur McCoy." She took his hand and led him past a painting of a swan and a naked woman having sex, to a round bed in the center of the sixty foot long room. She sat down and patted the spot beside her.

"We move the art pieces around for variety, but I have my favorites here near the passion center," she said.

Directly in front of them was a rough sculpture of a man's torso, his erect phallus in the face of a woman who had taken half of the rod into her mouth. Another marble statue standing beside it showed the buttocks of a fat woman with a penis about to penetrate her.

"Mr. McCoy, you haven't said a word. You do make love, don't you? You do like women and tits and cunts and sucking mouths?"

"Yes. It's such a surprise. It must have taken you years to gather all this."

"I have friends who help, who come here once a week. Six of us now, for group sex parties. I wanted to invite you but I thought slow and steady would be more appropriate at the beginning."

Celeste walked in, still darkly naked. She went on her knees behind Mrs. Engleton and began undressing her. It took only a few moments before the two women were naked.

Celeste moved to Spur, edged a breast toward his mouth. He kissed it. Both women cheered, then they undressed him.

They sat side by side on the bed, Spur still amazed at the variety of sexually explicit art around him.

"What is the sexiest thing you can think of, Mr. McCoy?" Mrs. Engleton asked.

Spur looked at them, stroked the breasts of each, surprised at the differences in the black and white, large and small. He thought about it a few seconds.

"At the moment the sexiest thing I can think of is watching you two make love to each other. But don't worry, I'll be a participant before too long."

Mrs. Engleton looked at her maid, who smiled. "Celeste, I don't think I have told you often enough how much I love you, how I enjoy having you here, how I am delighted with your compact, sexy body, and how I adore having your hands touch me." She lay down on the bed, closed her eyes, and Celeste bent over her, the girl's long, slender fingers barely touching the larger, white flattened breasts. Flying over the flesh, teasing, touching, moving away, leaving a wanting for more.

Mildred Engleton moaned softly. "Yes, yes!"

The touching continued, more and more contact was made until the black hands were fully engaged, stroking softly the large half orbs, then working harder around the big nipples, until they began to rise, harden and enlarge.

"Yes, darling Celeste. Oh, yes!" The larger woman rolled over and lifted to her hands and knees, letting her breasts hang downward swaying like two pendulums.

Celeste turned on her back, worked under the hanging mounds and began licking them gently. Her mouth worked around each breast, then lower and lower until the pulsating, hot nipple was drawn into her mouth and she chewed gently on it. As she sucked on the nipples, Mrs. Engleton jolted into a surging, shrieking climax. The walls bounced back her cries of satisfaction, and Spur wondered if they could not be heard outside.

As the climax wound down, Celeste pushed from under the white woman and sat on her back as a jockey would and with her left hand spanked Mrs. Engleton's fat round buttocks.

The wailing now had a note of pain in it as the woman reacted to the rougher sexual treatment, but this too brought on a climax that set her bucking and bouncing until the rider was thrown off, and both collapsed on the bed.

Now Celeste was facing the older woman's feet. She slowly pressed the white legs apart and with one hand smoothed the pubic hair over the nether lips. Slowly the caresses increased in tempo and force until at last Celeste's fingers parted the silky crotch hair and exposed her love nest.

With soft, gentle fingers, Celeste feather brushed the pubic area and around her crotch and then back as she came nearer and nearer to the sensitive, pink lips. When at last she touched them tenderly, Mrs. Engleton erupted in a long awaited climax and surged a dozen times with her hips as her whole body shook and vibrated and rattled as if it would never stop.

It was another two minutes before Mrs. Engleton quieted sufficiently for Celeste to find the tiny node, the joy trigger, the clit that she stroked back and forth.

At once Mrs. Engleton shivered and wailed in a different kind of a climax, one that started her crying with short potent sobs of joy-pain-relief-satisfaction all at once.

Suddenly Celeste pushed her face into the very center of Mrs. Engleton's nether lips, her tongue jamming in as deep as it would go. The white woman bellowed out in surprise and total joy. Celeste turned around, fell on the older woman and began humping her hips at the other's hips. Each picked up the rhythm and slammed against each other for two or three minutes before they whimpered again and again. Then the pumping slowed and stopped and they relaxed in each other's arms. For a moment they slept.

They woke up three minutes later, and Celeste jumped up and ran from the room.

Mrs. Engleton sat up and smiled at him. "Isn't she good? She is so delicious I'm afraid someone else will hire her away from me." Mrs. Engleton smiled. "Did you think that was sexy?"

"I've never seen anything so tender, so gentle, and so violently sexy all at the same time. I thought you were going to have a heart seizure."

"I almost did." She smiled. "Now it's my turn to please you. Whatever you want, however you want me, anything, just anything at all."

"I do like tits," Spur said. "Hang those two for me again and I'll pretend they are vanila cones of dessert!"

They made love twice, gently and with feeling, then Celeste brought in cheese, grapes and melons all cut into small squares and a variety of salted nuts. She put down the food and two bottles of wine and left quickly, by direction, Spur was sure. She was still naked.

After the snack they experimented trying to duplicate some of the poses they found in the art works, but they usually ended in a tangle of arms, legs and torsos.

It was just after three A.M. when Spur finished dressing and kissed Mrs. Engleton goodbye. As he did she pressed something into his hand.

"Don't look at it until you get back to your hotel," she said. "It's just a small gift so you'll remember me and this night. And when you're back in town again, you might send me a note asking about my art collection."

Spur nodded, kissed her again, and went out the big front door to his buggy in the street. He was glad it had been a dinner party for one, after all. Before he drove away he opened the small box she had given him and looked inside. He found a man's ring, a wide gold band set with black onyx surrounding a large diamond. He frowned as he looked at it. It must be at least a two carat diamond, and worth half a year's salary.

Was it a bribe or a gift? He frowned a moment, then grinned. It was simply a gift to a friend from a rich and oversexed lady.

CHAPTER EIGHT

Katherine Sanford had stopped telling her parents where she was going five years ago when she began going out nights. Tonight they were sleeping when she slipped out of the mansion, walked to her own small gray house three blocks away and changed quickly into her Kate uniform, baggy shirt and pants, hair on top of her head and the pinned on hat to turn her into a young man.

Tonight she drove a buggy she had left in back of the house earlier, and met her four gang members a block from the foundry and metal works owned by a Mr. Nelson. He was an elderly man, not much interested in his firm anymore, and there was no activity at all there after five o'clock. His night watchman was a poor man and for a twenty dollar gold piece he would help them come in and use the equipment, just as long as they didn't steal anything or break it.

Seven times they had been here, coming over a back fence, lugging in the various types of metal they had used for the stamping blanks and the gold to use in plating. Tonight things went according to plan.

Hop Choy was lookout near the street. If anyone came or if the police were about to disrupt the stamping, he would fire one shot in the air.

Tim Hackett was boss tonight. He was the expert die man who had created the dies and knew how to use them in a stamp press. He also handled the gold plating of the base metal stock. Tonight they had strips of copper two and a half inches wide and five feet long.

Tim had tried to explain the stamping process to Kate one night, but she couldn't wade through the details. He could do it, so she told him to do it.

He explained that they would use a method over two thousand years old, although the pressure may have been delivered in those days through the use of a crude sledgehammer. The upper and lower dies were embossed and engraved with the design of the double gold eagle. The metal blank was then fed to the lower die which was positioned securely on a solid base and with a knurled ring around it so the metal was confined and could not spread as the upper die was powered down on it with a great force.

It usually took Hackett about an hour to set up the stamping press with his dies and to get everything right. First the metal strips were fed into the press and the cutting die stamped out the individual coins. They had to be cut out first so the gold plating would coat the sides of the metal as well. Tim cut them with a die that was perfectly round and exactly the size of the double eagle and would even leave the required serration on the edges of the coins. After the blanks were plated they would be *struck off* with another hit of the stamping press to finish them. It was a two strike process.

When the press was set up correctly, Hackett got ready to plate the blanks. Tonight they had enough stock to strike up two hundred coins—if everything went right.

Breed prowled the outside of the buildings, watching, listening, looking for any trouble. Twice he rushed in and told everyone to remain silent as someone passed close by.

Foster Burke was along to carry stock and to help with his gun if there was any trouble which gave him time to talk to Kate.

Foss edged up beside Kate as she watched the plating process and put his hand on her shoulder.

"That was a terrific swim we had yesterday," he said.

She brushed his hand away, her eyes cold. "I don't remember anything about a swim, and you better not either. Today we have new work, new problems. We take care of today today."

"Yeah, sure, only I thought maybe tonight, after we're done here. . . ."

"No."

Foss cocked his head in surprise. "Just a flat no? Not even a maybe or a later, or something?"

"Just a no. I run this outfit, Foss, don't forget. I put it together, I paid the bills when you were knocking over stage coaches and going broke. It's my gang to do whatever I damn well please with. Without me you'd be back hustling whores on the Barbary Coast. Now, let's get these blanks moved over where we can get them into production."

"Yes, Ma'am!" Foss said with an exaggerated amount of snap and subservience.

Kate watched him go, wondering if her romp with him yesterday had been a good idea after all. He could think he was getting too important for his own good. She dismissed it and watched Jim Hackett cutting out the round blanks that would soon become double eagles. The coin blanks came from a strip of copper the correct thickness, two and a half inches wide and five feet long. They could cut out thirty coins from the strip.

When all two hundred and fifteen blanks had been cut out, Tim took them to the hot plating area and gold plated them, let them dry and then brought them back in racks.

Back at the press, Tim changed the dies, putting in those with the gold eagle engravings and began to *strike off* the actual coins.

They were done by four A.M. and Kate gave each of the men three coins and warned them.

"We must be careful where we spend these. I got one mixed up the other day and deposited it at a bank. They caught it and asked me where I got it. I told them at a store somewhere. We must spend these only at large stores that take in hundreds a day, then the clerks will not be able to remember who passes them. A small shop owner will remember."

They spent the next half hour taking the dies off the press and putting all the equipment back the way they had found it. By 4:30 they were across the fence and heading for their various houses. Hop Choy stayed at the little gray house in the city, Burke and the Breed were out at the ranch house and Tim Hackett had a wife and a small house in the north side of town.

Hop Choy drove the rig for her on the home trip. He also carried the 200 coins to the buggy. They had struck 215, so she had 203 to put in her hoard. Kate had made a fair profit for the night's work, four thousand dollars! She had an arrangement with Tim that every other time they struck off coins, he would get 25. It was payment for his work on the dies and his expertise. The others were satisfied with their sixty dollars. That was two months' wages for most factory workers and laborers.

Before Breed rode away, she told him to stop by at the little house. He nodded and left.

She wondered about Breed, his Indian blood, his savage redskin mother. Would he be different? She shivered. It would be exciting finding out.

A half hour later she removed a section of the floor boards in the back bedroom and lowered the heavy sack into the hidden vault-like safe she had created there. The house could burn down and not harm the gold. She looked in her small notebook and made an entry. Now she had a few over two thousand of the coins! They had spent another three hundred perhaps. Her goal was fifty thousand dollars. She could have that in three more strikings!

She would start her deposits of four hundred dollars in various small banks around town, then transfer the credits after a month or so to one bank, and the counterfeit coins would be washed clean and pure. No one could trace them, and her credits in her main bank would be secure!

She was thrilled at the thought. Fifty thousand dollars all her own, that she had made herself. She didn't care if her father was rich, if he was worth five million dollars. This was money she had earned herself!

Hop Choy went to the back door and let in Breed. She covered up the safe and put the rug back, then sat on the bed and called to Breed to come back. He stepped inside the room, his dark eyes darting a quick look at her shirt. He was a man all right.

She closed the door and began talking. It would relax him, make him more sure of himself.

"Breed, I know you said once your name was Tom, may I call you that? It will be so much better." She closed the door and began unbuttoning her shirt. "Tom, could you help me with these buttons?" He nodded and unfastened them, then pushed the shirt off her shoulders and frowned at the tight wrapper she had put around her breasts to flatten them for her disguise.

Kate laughed. "Yes, Tom, I do have breasts, I

had to hide them. Here, unwrap this for me." He did and her breasts lifted and she shook them and Tom's eyes glowed.

"Tom, I don't think we're going to have any trouble at all. I do hope it hasn't been a long time for you. Remember you must be soft and gentle."

Breed bent and sucked half of one of her big breasts into his mouth and began chewing on it.

"No, Tom, I don't think we're going to have any problems at all this first time."

Outside the small gray house, Foss Burke settled down beside a box in the alley. He rolled a smoke and watched the horse that Breed rode. The back bedroom light had stayed on in the little house, and he could imagine Breed kneeling over that glorious white meat and lunging forward, taking her and making her like it just the way Burke had done three times yesterday.

Foss grinned. Yes sir, a man could take orders from a woman for just so long, then there came a time to settle up. He knew all about the floor safe and how to get into it. He figured she must have sixty, maybe seventy thousand dollars worth of counterfeit double eagles in there by now. Hell, with money like that a man could hole up in some little town and live as top dog for the rest of his natural life. Just take some careful *investing* in small banks and then getting letters of credit when he moved on.

The only problem was the timing. Things were going so damn smooth right now. She put another two thousand dollars worth away tonight.

Shit! He should do it tonight!

He could rent a rig, give Hop Choy the choice of going with them, or taking a .44 slug in the gut. Then him and Breed could light out with the gold in the buggy and live high on the hog!

Foss snorted. Damned if he almost talked himself into it. But not quite. He wanted like crazy to have another go round with that sweet little pussy. Breed was getting his tonight. Foss should come due in another week. She was always hot to get punched. It gave her some wild thrill to play at being a damned outlaw. He'd seen other women react that way. One night a woman *knew* that he had robbed a stage outside of town that afternoon and it got him the best piece of ass he'd ever had. The woman had gone crazy because he was laying her.

Foss knew who Kate was, a Sanford for Christ's sakes. She could buy and sell half the merchants in town. Her father was good for maybe ten million dollars!

No chance to marry into that kind of money, but he was going to get one more good fuck into it before he took off with her little stash of coins!

Fuck away, Katherine Sanford, you have met your match in Foster Burke, he thought. She just didn't know it yet.

CHAPTER NINE

Spur woke up the next morning at 6:30 as usual, put on his light blue suit and flat heeled boots. He felt like a wet dishrag that had been drawn and quartered. He rinsed his mouth out with a swallow from the china pitcher on the wash stand slicked back his hair and went down the back stairs for a walk down to the waterfront and back.

That got his blood circulating and his mind in gear. Without thinking about it he suddenly remembered the name and problems of the gunman who had tried to put holes in his hide yesterday.

Rich Turneau was a small time counterfeiter from St. Louis. Spur had sent him to prison four years ago. He was a one man operation then, dealing in five dollar bills. He had used poor plates and he was not a good counterfeiter or passer.

Could Rich have developed into a big timer? Doubtful, Spur decided, but possible. At least it was a solid lead. But how to find Rich? Why not let Rich find him . . . again? At the same time if he let Rich find him, there had to be a plan not to get suddenly dead.

Spur went into the San Franciscan by the side door, charged to the dining room and ordered a breakfast of six eggs and bacon, three slices of toast and two cups of coffee.

Upstairs he went to room 310 and dug out his gunbelt and cleaned and oiled his .44. Today should prove interesting.

Just after 9 A.M. Spur brought his rig around to the front of the hotel, had a boy carry a big empty box out to the buggy and made a fuss about getting it in the rig just right, then sent the boy away laughing with a dollar bill in his hand.

The scene was designed to make sure that Rich Turneau saw Spur and knew that he was leaving. Nobody could have slept through that performance.

Spur drove south, the quickest way out of the built up area and toward the low brown hills. He made sure that he did not obviously look to the rear, but twice he caught glimpses of a rig a hundred yards behind him. Both times it was the same one. Spur made a detour down a side road and then back to the main track south, and his black topped Democrat buggy was still with him.

Soon they had passed the houses, and Spur noticed an occasional small ranch and small farm. The road leveled out, then turned toward the coast,

and just as Spur made the turn he heard a rifle shot. His horse stumbled and went down. The buggy crashed into the animal, almost tipped over and then settled on its wheels. One final scream of fear bellowed from the mare before she lifted her head and died in the traces.

Rich was getting serious. Spur jumped out of the buggy away from the other rig and sprinted in a zig zag course into a small clump of live oak trees and brush. He couldn't see anyone in the buggy behind him, but it had stopped in the road.

Spur edged around a tree and watched the black rig. It moved as if a person were getting in or out. It began rolling forward, but no driver, no one was visible. It was a moving blind, a protective cover for the ambusher.

Now Spur wished that he had his seven shot Spencer rifle along. He would make short work of this attacker, but as it was the other man had the advantage. He had a long gun, he was on the offensive, and he had murder in mind.

The Democrat buggy kept coming. When it was opposite the point where McCoy had entered the woods, it stopped. He heard a voice.

"Spur McCoy, you stupid bastard, you better start thinking about dying, 'cause that's what you're going to be doing before this day is over. Christ, but I've waited a long time for this."

As soon as he stopped talking a shotgun boomed and Spur jerked his head back behind the big oak, as half a dozen big slugs hit the tree and the brush around him. Double-ought buck!

He knew how well it killed, but he had never been on the receiving end before. Nine to thirteen .33 caliber sized slugs packed into a three-inch shotgun shell. Two rounds was like having ten men each firing two shots at you with a .32 caliber revolver.

So Rich had a rifle, a shotgun and probably a pistol. Spur was tempted to put a round through the soft canvas top of the buggy, but decided he had better save his ammunition. He had only the five in his weapon and eighteen in the belt loops.

"You get out of prison legal, or you bust out, Turneau?"

"Parole, and I learned plenty inside. The first thing I learned was to wipe out the sonofabitch who jailed me, and that's you, Spur, and you're as good as dead. I've got plenty of ammunition, how much do you have?"

Spur aimed carefully with the .44 and slammed a round through the canvas low and he hoped just over the seat. Before the sound of the round had echoed away, he was up and moving through the woods, deeper into it, running hard before Rich realized he had left. Principal number one here was to get the enemy away from his rolling fortress and ammunition supply. If he had to carry a shotgun and a rifle and a pistol, he would have less room for additional ammunition.

As Spur ran he heard Rich say something behind him but he didn't stop to listen. He ran as silently as possible, without smashing branches or snapping brush. He took a route that went gradually down a slope and merged into a small brush filled creek.

Knowing that Rich would come after him, he needed a protected ambush spot, where he could lure Rich to within twenty yards without Rich realizing it was a trap.

It was the only way Spur could take on the shotgun and rifle and have any hope of living more than a few more hours. He heard the shotgun roar again near the road, then the crack of a heavy long gun, maybe a Sharps.

He needed rocks for protection, but there were no boulders on these smooth, sparsely wooded San Francisco rolling hills. The high ground? He looked around and saw a stretch of timber that climbed to the left up to the highest point around. He ran again, working through the heavier brush and trees toward the top of the small hill. The live oak were thick here, and many of them were old when Columbus discovered the New World.

Spur lay behind one at the brow of the slope and looked around its three foot diameter at the land below.

After ten minutes he saw a figure moving carefully through the woods. The day had turned hot, the humidity was low, and the sun burning down.

He watched the hunter below. He was good, not taking any chances, moving from cover to cover. For a moment Spur thought he might be able to circle behind him, get to the road and take the Democrat buggy and drive for town. But then Rich moved laterally a hundred yards and swung back. He too had thought of that and would cut off any try.

Spur settled down to wait. Rich could not track

him, he wasn't even watching the ground. He was guessing, and so far his logic had been as good as Spur's. Now if he chose the high ground and started up. . . .

Spur looked to his left and could see the ocean. Close by long dry grass covered many areas. It would provide no protection. The dry wind came again and Spur was surprised at its heat. It was one of those hot winds that come off the California deserts and blow toward the sea, a Santa Ana, the natives called them.

When Spur saw Rich come through a small stand of live oak and brush he could tell that the man was tracking him. Spur had made no attempt not to leave a trail or to conceal it. Rich had more talent at tracking than making counterfeit ten dollar bills.

Rich was still a hundred yards away. Much too far for Spur's .44, but easy range for a rifle. He looked around at his alternatives. His forehead sweated as he considered them. He could turn and run down the hill toward the beach a half mile over, but what good would that do? He still needed that ambush chance, but now the possibility seemed to be growing less all the time.

Circle back to the Democrat buggy? That was one good chance. A run for it? What else? A do or die ambush behind a big oak tree, allowing Rich to walk right up to him in good pistol range.

It wasn't just a case of run or fight. Spur would have to go across two open places to get back to the buggy. Rich would have a clear shot at him, probably six or seven shots. He should not miss with those odds.

So it was stand and fight. He ran down the hill fifty yards and found the tree he needed. It was live oak, with shiny green leaves that stayed on the trees all year round. New leaves grew all year replacing those that dropped off. This one was four feet across, ancient, scraggly, partly dead, but with plenty of bulk to hide him and offer a good shooting fort. To one side there was a hole all the way through the trunk, probably carved out in some long forgotten grass fire.

The growth up hill from the big tree was young, nothing big enough to hide behind. Rich would have to stand and fight.

It was several minutes before Rich came over the crest of the hill. He stood up from behind a small bush where he had been watching the downslope. He was good. Spur had been under cover all the time. There was no chance Rich could know where Spur was, or whether he was hiding or running. Rich would watch the big tree with caution, probably walk well to one side of it as he passed.

Spur would be edging around it until he could get his shot. He had to be on target with the first one. Now Spur noticed that Rich did not carry the shotgun. That was one less weapon to deal with. He had two six-guns on his hips, however.

McCoy waited. The odds in this match were not in his favor. He had to do everything right, do it lightning fast and be dead on target.

Rich came forward twenty yards and stopped. He stood near a downed oak that would give him good cover, if he needed it. Ahead there was no cover. Spur watched him from the base of the tree through some two foot high squawbush.

Rich loosened the six-gun on his right, and made sure there was a round in the long gun, then he moved ahead, slowly, angling away to his right around the big oak. He glanced at it each step, then swept the land in front of him on the downgrade to the thick growth of cottonwoods and scrub oak. Behind the oak, Spur had the six-gun up and leveled, braced with both hands and ready to lean out, refine his arm and fire.

Rich was still thirty yards away, too far. A lucky shot might save him, but Spur could not rely on that. To Spur's surprise, Rich lowered the rifle, held it with his left hand and pulled his six-shooter from the right holster and thumbed back the hammer.

Why? A ruse to get Spur out in the open, then use the long gun? Probably. Rich had already shot at him twice from ambush, he wouldn't hesitate to use any dirty trick he could think of. Spur stayed where he was.

Twenty-five yards away.

Not yet. Spur wiped sweat from his forehead, peered through the brush again.

Suddenly Rich was running, not toward the tree, but at an angle around and past it. He had been twenty yards toward it, now he was twenty-five. Spur lifted up, stepped out, pulled down in a dead aim at the running man and fired three times. He saw the first two rounds miss. He saw Rich turn, surprised, and whip off two shots.

Spur's third shot had hit Rich in the right leg above the knee and he tumbled into the dirt and rolled. But Rich had fired his third shot and Spur felt the hammer blow to his left shoulder and saw himself thrown backward, behind the protection of the big oak.

He almost dropped the gun. His left shoulder was on fire. The bullet had gone in high, near the bone. It throbbed like the time he spilled bacon fat on his hand, only this was ten times worse. Spur watched the blood soak his jacket sleeve and then drip off his left hand. He had to stop it. First he lifted himself up and looked past the tree to the spot where Rich had been. He lay in a small depression. Spur could see only part of his back.

With a great deal of effort, Spur moved and stood up. He had a better angle on the counterfeiter. Spur aimed by resting the six-gun against the oak. He fired, but dug up dirt in front of the blue shirt. Rich moved so he could see none of him.

Sweating and swearing softly, Spur used his right hand and pulled the four fired rounds from his gun and pushed in four cartridges from his belt loops.

Then he took off his blue coat so he could look at his wound. His knife sliced through the hole in the shirt fabric, and he saw the black hole where the bullet had entered just below his collar bone almost under his arm. He didn't think that the lead slug came out. It bled more as he watched. How could he get a bandage on it? He cut off the sleeve of his shirt and folded part of it into a compress. Then he cut strips from the rest and clumsily tied them together.

Every half minute he leaned out and looked through the brush at the spot where Rich had dropped. Nothing.

He pushed the compress in place with his hand, then held it there with his chin as he looped the strips of cloth over his shoulder and under his arm and tied them with loose double overhand knots. Good enough, it would stay in place for a while. He discarded his coat and stood, lifting himself as high as he could. He could make out the edge of some brown cloth.

Was Rich still there? Had he faked the wound and circled around to zero in on Spur with the rifle? Spur stepped on part of the burned, hollowed section of the oak and boosted himself up another three feet. Now he looked through a crotch in the ancient tree. Rich Turneau lay exactly where Spur thought he had.

"Turneau, you might as well give it up. You'll never get away from here with a shot up leg. Throw out your weapons, all four of them, including the hide-out, and I'll help you back to the buggy. You'll still have to face an assault with a deadly weapons charge."

His answer came in a rifle shot that slammed less than two inches over Spur's partly revealed head. He dropped down. Strategy. Spur was mobile; he wasn't sure how active Rich could be.

Should he get away or end it here, Spur wondered? He could angle away from Rich, up the hill where Rich couldn't see him or shoot at him. But then Rich would still be trying later to kill Spur. He had to end it now, one way or the other.

But how? Spur wished he had some of those half-stick dynamite bombs he had made from time to time. They would be perfect. He could make a small bomb with all the black powder from his remaining pistol rounds, but that would leave him out of ammunition.

Burn him out? Yes, the wind was right, but it also would burn all the way to the coast and could easily sweep north into San Francisco. Not a good idea.

Circle.

Spur looked where Rich was down, then looked away up the hill in a direct line with the tree and Rich. The rifleman could not see him for forty yards, then he would have ten yards to cross before Rich saw him or got a shot off. The odds were the best he had all day. He pressed the bandage on his shoulder again, gripped his shirt front with his left hand, turned and ran hard on the one line of retreat that was safe.

Spur looked back as he passed the small tree he figured was the end of his cover. He could not see Rich. Digging in his boots he bolted the last ten yards and got over the top of the ridge.

Automatically he swung left, to go downhill and circle so he could come out in the heavier woods below and have a good view of the low place where Rich should still be hiding.

No one lay on the hillside.

Rich had done exactly the same thing Spur had. Only he must have moved much slower away from his spot, using the tree as his cover, hoping Spur wouldn't look out just then.

Spur lined up the two positions and moved silently

through the trees toward the spot Rich could have
entered the thicker growth. He found the spot
something dragging, perhaps a broken leg, then he
spotted dark red stains of blood on a leaf. Where
ahead could Rich be?

He would try for the buggy. That was the key
now. Spur angled away from the shortest route back
to the road and the transportation. He circled
slightly to the left through heavy woods and came
out on the road two hundred yards toward San Francisco from the rig. No one was there.

Spur crawled through the grass working silently
and he hoped unseen toward the buggy. Five
minutes later he was within thirty yards of the rig.
He raised himself to search the route from woods to
buggy but saw no one. Spur eased back down and
waited.

Twenty minutes later he heard a soft groan of
agony from ahead. He lifted himself up but saw no
one. Then he realized that Rich was crawling
through the grass too, not to stay unobserved, but
because he probably couldn't walk.

The sounds came closer.

Spur waited.

The sounds changed, Rich turned. He was almost
to the buggy.

The shotgun! Spur should have found the shotgun
and had it as his second weapon. Too late.

Rich eased out of the grass and reached for the
buggy wheel to help himself stand up.

Spur put a slug into the side of the buggy over
Rich's head.

"That's far enough, Rich. Hold it right there."

Two pistol shots blasted toward Spur but they had no target, finding only grass and dirt.

"That won't help you, Rich. You have no target. I have a big one. Shall I try for you this time?"

"I won't go back to prison. I'll die first."

"Talking that way you will. Throw down the pistols and the rifle."

"I don't have the rifle, dropped it back there, before I started crawling."

"Drop them."

Rich shrugged. "What the hell, prison is better than dead. You win, McCoy." He leaned against the buggy wheel with his back, let the six-gun fall into the dirt. "You win."

Spur stood, leveled the gun at Rich and walked forward. He stumbled in the grass, almost fell but caught himself, bringing a scream of pain as he jerked his arm around suddenly.

When he looked back at Rich he saw a six-gun firing. Spur fired four times, and saw three of the heavy slugs pound into the counterfeiter's chest, smearing it with blood and slamming him against the wheel, then to the ground under the rig. He was dead before he hit the ground.

Spur moved up cautiously. The counterfeiter's eyes were glazed, there was no pulse. The gun remained frozen in Rich Turneau's hand in a death grip.

It took Spur ten minutes to get the body lifted into the buggy. His shoulder burned now, every small movement dug daggers into the wound. Lifting the dead body was excruciating.

He turned the buggy around and drove back to town, to the police station, showed them his thin Secret Service identification card taped between two photos of his parents, and at last the police understood. The livery sent someone out the south road to cut the horse loose and to bring back the buggy. Spur had to pay forty dollars for the dead horse and another five dollars for bringing back the buggy.

"It figures," Spur said. "Now they'll probably have both spinach and eggplant on the menu at the hotel dining room." He was wrong. They only had spinach.

CHAPTER TEN

Police Captain Vuylsteke had looked at Spur's shoulder and recommended a doctor who was good with bullets. The sawbones had given Spur a long smell of chloroform, and he entered an amazing world where everything was strange and funny. He was almost unconscious and couldn't feel a thing.

For an hour after it was over he kept asking the doctor when he was going to start taking out the bullet. Then Spur came fully conscious and saw his arm in a sling, his shoulder bandaged and a feeling that his main assignment was all shot to hell.

"You'll be as good as new in two weeks," the doctor said. "Go home, and stay in bed for a week. Then come see me again."

Spur nodded gravely and got outside as soon as he could. Captain Vuylsteke said he would send two men to Turneau's address which they had found in his wallet. Spur had insisted on going along before he went to the doctor. In the rooming house they found plates for five and ten dollar bills, and some new ones that Turneau was working on for twenties. In his belongings they found over ten thousand dollars in counterfeit bills and about five hundred in double eagles. He evidently had been passing the bills and converting them into gold.

Back in his hotel room, Spur had stripped and washed as best he could in the china bowl, then put on a clean suit and took a cab to the Sanford residence. The butler seemed surprised to see him. When he asked to talk to Katherine, the man frowned and asked Spur to wait in the library.

It was a half hour before Katherine came in. She looked at his injured arm.

"What in the world have you done? Injured yourself seriously it looks like. Whatever am I to do with you men. Always showing off and hurting yourselves. Well, we'll just have to take your mind off your hurt. It's a glorious day, much too nice to stay in town, let's go sailing on the bay."

"I know nothing of boats, Miss Sanford."

"Silly, you don't have to, neither do I. It's father's boat and he has a crew to sail it. All we have to do is enjoy the wind and the water. It will be delightful. Cook will send ahead a nice lunch for us. You simply can't say no."

"I'm not supposed to get this wet," he said showing her his arm.

She touched it and smiled. "We won't get wet at all. How did you hurt it?"

"I could tell you i got drunk and fell down. I could say one of the wild San Francisco fancy ladies bit me. Actually I got shot."

"If you don't want to tell me, fine. Today I want to enjoy life and have fun. I'll have some things from my room and see you right back here in two minutes. My carriage is in back."

Her driver took them to Bay Street where several docks held small sailing boats. Small compared to ocean going clipper ships, but much larger than Spur had ever seen privately owned. The Sanford boat was forty-five feet long, had twin masts, and more lines and ropes and cables than he had seen before.

"This is it, the *Francisco Belle*. She's not new, but she sails well."

Two men in sailor blues and wearing white hats met her at the rail and helped her on board. She shook hands and talked to them a minute.

"Just around the bay, and no fishing. We have an important meeting to take care of so please don't disturb us. I'll let you know when we want to dock again."

She took Spur's right hand and gave him the guided tour. Below there were two cabins forward, a galley and dining area amidships, and a large captain's cabin aft. The big cabin had a full sized bed, dressers built into the walls, a gas lamp and all the comforts of a luxurious living room and bedroom.

Spur felt the ship tremble as it edged away from the dock. Then it quivered as the sails went up and caught the wind.

"Let's go up and watch us moving out," Katherine

said. "This is the exciting part of sailing."

The men scurried around the deck, hoisting sail, working out through incoming ships. They lifted another sail that billowed out in the afternoon breeze. At the helm a seaman turned the rudder and they angled half into the wind toward the inland side of the bay. Katherine took a deep breath. "The salt spray is so invigorating! I just love to sail." She turned and went below to the big cabin and Spur followed.

As soon as the door closed, Spur caught her with his right arm and pulled her gently to him. When he bent to kiss her she was ready. His lips clung to hers as he rubbed her back, then he let go of her and his right hand wormed between their bodies until he found her breasts. She moaned softly.

"Yes, beautiful man! Oh, yes! Sailing just sets me on fire! I don't know what it is, but as soon as we start sailing I want to tear off my clothes and attack anything with a pecker." She giggled and helped him as he unbuttoned the top of her dress.

She kissed him again, her tongue barging inside his mouth, fighting him, licking his teeth, searching for his tongue. Her arms wrapped around him so tightly that it made his arm throb, but Spur didn't mind. His blood was boiling and he pushed his hips hard against her pubic center to show her. She murmured deep in her throat and stepped back so that his hand could find her nearly bare breasts.

"You like my tits, don't you, Spur?"

"Yes, they are perfect and so big I want to try to eat them up."

The boat turned and slanted and they both fell on the bed giggling.

She rolled on top of him, pushed her dress down so her breasts hung out. She moved upward and one dangled deliciously over his face.

"Now, beautiful man, now you can try to chew me flat busted."

Spur's mouth closed around the heavy nipple and sucked in more of it and she yelped when he bit her.

"Easy, dammit! I was just kidding about chewing me off. Nibble but don't bite!"

Spur laughed and moved his right arm, then went back to his feast of hanging tits.

As she let him suck and chew, she found his fly and opened the buttons, working inside until she caught his erection.

"Now there is something worth getting fucked with," she said and laughed. "I don't know why it makes me feel wicked to say fucked. It's just another word. Fuck, fuck, fuck. As in I'm going to fuck you!" She tittered. "It still makes me feel naughty."

"I may recuperate here all day and all night," Spur said between bites. "This is good therapy for my arm."

"And it will be a shrinking therapy for your long, hot cock," she said.

They both laughed.

She gently rubbed his erection and watched him eating her breasts.

"I don't understand most women. They try to act so aloof and pure, like the only reason they *ever* let their husbands have their way with them is to produce children. Dammit, women *like to fuck* as much as men do. Some women have to get warmed up to the idea, but they love it. They say they don't, but I heard my women relatives talking one night, three of them, women in their thirties, all married, all with four or five kids each. They began talking about fucking, which they called *doing it*. I have never heard a sexier, explicit talk about making love.

"The way I look at it, all women are whores. Most of them don't get in bed with a man until they get him to marry them, that's supposed to be the big prize, their wet little pussy. But then they fuck away, give it away, but in return they work at it, doing his clothes, raising his kids, taking his money. How are they any different from the girls down in the red light district who give you men your two dollars worth and push you out the door? The married woman just gets her security and her keep in a different form of payoff."

She rolled over beside him, lifted his erection from his pants and sighed.

"A cock is the most beautiful thing in the world, did you know that, McCoy? It is. Look at him. Straight and tall, and pink and purple and throbbing with life, wanting to spread life." She pushed her hand lower and gently picked up his scrotum. "Of course your balls are fucking important too."

She sat up and waited for him to sit. The boat rocked and she nodded. "When the boat rolls when we're fucking you won't believe the new, wild sensation." She stopped and stared at him. "The other night you said the next time would be long and slow.

Good! This is it. I want you to undress me, slow and easy, kissing every part of my clothes off, just kissing me all over!" She shivered. "Then, beautiful man, when I'm all naked, I'll kiss off your clothes and we'll see how long we can hold off before we have to fuck each other or explode!"

Spur pushed her down on her back, kissed her lips to softly she hardly felt him. He worked down her cheek and chin and her neck to her breasts, where he anointed each one and moved to her shoulder where he pushed off the fabric kissing it down as he went.

"Oh, yes, Spur! That is heaven, so soft and gentle, so easy and relaxing. Yes. Did I tell you my one big dream, Sweet Man Spur? What I really want to do more than anything else is to take this boat and the crew of two and sail her to Hawaii. Then I want to stay there. Just sit in the sand and play, and fuck the big Hawaiians when they want to, and swim naked in the warm waters and walk around without any top on all the time. I have heard that they are extremely casual about sex and that children often belong to everyone because they are not really sure who the father is."

Spur pushed the dress fabric lower off her arms and lifted her up and pulled it off her back bunching it around her waist.

He kissed down across her breasts again to her soft stomach and worked down to her waist.

"Now this is getting more interesting," she said. "I wonder if he has guts enough to kiss down any further."

Spur pulled the fabric down more. He was sure

the dress was supposed to slip over her head, but he was too far down to change directions. He pulled the fabric over her hips, caught the top of her under drawers and worked them down over her soft belly until he saw fringes of pubic hair.

He stopped and kissed rings and squares and designs on her flat tummy and moved down, ever down to the soft dark hair. She began trembling as he pushed the cloth lower, kissing as he went. He circled around the pinkness showing through the silky black crotch hair.

Katherine was moaning now, her legs twitching, her hips grinding against the mattress. Spur shoved the clothing down to her knees and pushed his face into her pubic hair, kissing down farther, circling her glory spot and then reaching down and parting the forest of dark hair to expose the wet, pulsing pinkness of her nether lips.

"Now, Spur, fuck me now!"

He ignored her, saw her hips rotating, then pumping up gently and retreating, then coming high again. He worked in closer, kissed her wet, steaming nether lips and she exploded with a scream and a sharp series of tremors that shook her body. Her cries came again and again, and her hips went wild with gyrations. She moaned and bounced and swore and cried and at last shuddered to a stop. Only then did her eyes come open. She brushed joy-tears away and stared at him.

"God, nobody ever did that for me before, actually kissed my pussy! I think I am in heaven. Do that twice more and I'll kill my parents, inherit all the money and marry you!'"

She panted and he smiled, watching her.

"That was wonderful, marvelous. It's the best one I've ever had. I thought I was going to break in half and die right here on the bed. God, what a fucking good feeling, and your prick wasn't even inside me! It's going to be a half hour before I'm anywhere near back to normal. If I dressed and said hello to somebody, anybody, they would grin and know that I had just had the fuck of my life!"

"We can't let you get back to normal, then, can we?" Spur said. He pulled the tangled clothes off her feet and threw them on the floor. He lifted her to the center of the big bed and kissed her breasts, then dropped to her pubic hair and kissed around her heartland. When she started to gasp in anticipation, he kissed her nether lips again, tasting the soft fluid that came out, and kissed her again, then flicked out his tongue to strike her clit and Katherine exploded. She lifted upward, humping him high, then she bellowed a scream that Spur was sure would bring the crew running, but no one banged on the locked door.

When her screaming faded she mumbled over and over.

"Omigod, Omigod, Omigod. I'm dying. I'm dying!" The spasms shot through her, shattering her whole body with trembling and jolting and shaking until she seemed one moving mass of flesh.

It was almost five minutes before she tapered off, and the spasms stopped.

He kissed her lips and she smiled. Spur realized that she was almost asleep.

"Don't touch me, I'm dead and I'm in heaven

right now." She smiled again, curled up into a fetal ball and went to sleep. She was awake almost at once.

"My God! You did it again. When are we going to get married? I want that every night for the rest of my life. I'll keep you in luxury, you can have six mistresses if you want just so you eat me every night!"

Spur chuckled. "I've heard it just gets better and better."

She looked at him and saw that he was slipping out of his clothes.

"You haven't even been in me yet and I feel like I've had the best fuck of my life."

"You're young yet, Katherine, so very young."

She lay on her back, spread her legs and lifted her knees and held out her arms to him. Spur was more than ready. He went to her with a sudden need, with a moment of knowing that he should have a wife and settle down, that he should stop all this cuntmongering, but also knowing that he wasn't likely to for a long time. With that in mind he bent and thrust into her with one sharp move that brought a cry of pain and desire and satisfaction from Katherine.

His own surging climax was an anticlimax to the tremendous exhibition Katherine had shown him. They lay there panting for a few minutes and she held him tightly.

"Let's have a little nap," she said. "It feels so safe, so warm and protected with you on top of me this way. Just a short little nap."

She was sleeping almost before he agreed, drifting off to a pleasant and he imagined dream filled few minutes.

Five minutes later Spur moved and she woke up.

"Wake up time, everyone," she said. "I'm hungry. I had some food sent on board before we got here." She stood and moved with the same erect, proud carriage he had seen on the dance floor. Most of Spur's women had been self-conscious when naked and could not move gracefully when unclothed. But Katherine's self-esteem enabled her to move just as beautifully naked as dressed.

Katherine went to a small cupboard and brought out three kinds of cheeses, four small melons, all different varieties, and a bottle of white wine.

"You thought of everything," he said.

"I try. Do you know that you're the first man I've ever made love with on two different days?"

"Curious. You like variety?"

"Yes, and I don't want to be tied down. Men get so possessive. If I fucked one three or four times, in three or four weeks he would assume we were going to be married."

"So for you it's simply recreation, a sport, a kind of intimate game to play, to strike back at convention, at the mores of our society, at the idea that women can't enjoy sex before marriage."

"Exactly. You sound like my college professors."

"Did you take any of them to bed?"

She laughed. "My philosophy professor stole my virginity, and it cost him an 'A' grade in his course. He kept trying but I wouldn't get near him again. I was too busy after that with college boys to bother with older men. The boys were so much more active."

Spur cut the melons. They ate melon and salted

119

nuts, drank the wine.

"Where did you get all these cheeses? I love good cheese."

"It's made locally up the coast somewhere." She stretched, one arm high, the other low, her breasts straining forward, thrust out to their maximum. Spur grinned.

"Now that is a beautiful picture. I wish I were an artist, I'd paint you in that pose."

She did it again, and he reached out and kissed the forward thrusting breasts.

"You are amazing, Katherine Sanford. A marvelous body, great tits, lovely shoulders, a flat little tummy and no waist at all, gently rounded hips and legs so slender and perfect that they take my breath away."

"I like you, let's fuck again."

They laughed.

"And all this long black hair. I love to get tangled up in it when I undress you."

"You should undress me more. Want me to come to your hotel room late tonight?"

"No, I couldn't satisfy your insatiable appetites. I'm not sixteen anymore with unlimited climaxes available."

She laughed. "I bet you caught your first little girl before you were sixteen."

"Somewhere around there, but she was nothing like you." He kissed her breasts again. They finished the wine and half the cheese. Then she stood to put away the things. Her reticule spilled from the side of the bed and a dozen gold double eagles rolled onto the floor. Spur dropped to the deck which had a soft carpet over it, and began picking them up. One caught his eye and then another. He thought he noticed the small peculiarity he had seen on the counterfeit coins. He palmed one of them as he put them back in her purse. When he picked up their clothes, he slid the coin into his pants pocket. He would check it later.

"Hey, let's go on deck and watch the water."

"Like this?"

"No, silly. We'll get dressed."

"Can I watch you dress? It's a very special spectacle watching a lady dress."

She shrugged. "If you like. I don't take long. Race you!"

They dressed and went on deck. The afternoon sun was still high and the boat had worked well down the southern half of the thirty-mile long San Francisco bay. The water was blue, the sky the same shade and the wind brisk as the boat sliced through the bay waters. A large clipper ship came into the bay to the north of them, and they saw how big it looked. It swung into a berth at the San Francisco harbor.

The bay was dotted with fishing craft and a few pleasure boats. Few people could afford boats to play with, and those who could usually didn't have time to sail just for the enjoyment. Katherine was an exception.

They moved in close across the bay and almost touched at a green park-like area on the mainland side, then swung around.

Spur wished he could stop beside some of the fishing boats and get on board for a few hours, but he knew that now wasn't the time. Perhaps later.

Katherine signalled the crew that it was time to head back to their berth, and the sailing craft turned into the wind and they began tacking back toward the San Francisco docks.

Spur had found that he could move his arm more freely now. He took it out of the sling and realized that the movement from his elbow down did not hurt the wound at all. There was no reason to continue using the sling.

An hour later they docked and left the boat. Katherine thanked the crew and gave each a double eagle. Spur wondered if they were real or counterfeit.

Spur turned down an invitation to dinner, explaining that he had to see two artists' work. She argued with him and at last gave up.

"But I do want to see you again tomorrow. Perhaps we could drive out into the country on a picnic, up along the coast somewhere. I'll bring a blanket and some lunch."

"I hate to say no, but I'm not sure. I'll send a note over in the morning one way or the other."

She dropped him off in front of his hotel with a formal handshake and was gone.

Spur stood watching the buggy roll away. He took the double eagle from his pocket and pricked the back with his pocket knife. The gold flaked away showing base metal underneath. It was counterfeit. He stared after the buggy. To have so many of them, she must somehow be involved. Exactly how she was tied into the ring would be his next assignment.

CHAPTER ELEVEN

The coffee was still hot a half hour after the waitress at the hotel restaurant had fixed Spur's dinner to take out. He had ordered two ham and cheese sandwiches, an apple and a quart mason jar full of coffee. She had wrapped the jar with a hotel towel to help it stay warm.

He sipped the coffee and looked for the millionth time at the two doors. He had parked his buggy in a position where he could see both the front and the side doors to the Sanford mansion. As far as he could tell there was no regularly used door leading into the alley. The house sat on a corner and the side door opened to a walk leading to a sparsely traveled side street.

McCoy had nothing more than a hunch. Katherine was stubborn, she was strong willed, she had not been welcomed into the management level at the store her father owned, and she was a real sexual rebel. Why not a counterfeiter too? She had been caught depositing a counterfeit coin. Granted that could happen to anyone if there were hundreds of them in circulation. But the dozen or so coins that Spur spotted in Katherine's purse were probably counterfeits. This led him to new and tougher conclusions.

Now all he had to do was try to prove if she was working some scheme, it most surely would be done either in some disguise or during the night. Perhaps both. The front door opened and a couple he assumed were Mr. and Mrs. Sanford came out. They went to the curb where their driver waited with a fancy carriage.

Lights came on in the house at dusk. Spur moved his rig a half block closer. The side door was not lighted by any windows. If she left, he guessed it would be by the side door.

By nine that night Spur's coffee was gone, both the sandwiches had vanished and he had eaten one of the apples. This might be a fool's errand after all. The poor sex crazed girl was probably no more than a nymphomaniac. He knew for certain that she qualified for that title.

Another hour and Spur found himself nodding. It was by a stroke of luck that he didn't miss her. His horse grew tired of the stationary position and jolted the rig ahead six feet, bringing Spur out of a doze. He shook his head and checked the side door just as a shaft of weak yellow light stabbed out as the door came open, then disappeared quickly. A shadow in a black coat and large hat left the house, walked quickly to the street and down the hill toward the lower priced houses of San Francisco. Spur had no way of telling who it was, but the steps were short, the stature about five-five, and the carriage . . . Yes! it was Katherine. There was no hiding that proud walk, chin high, shoulders back, chest out stance that had first caught his attention on the dance floor.

Katherine Sanford was going for a walk at 10 P.M. when *nice* girls were home in bed with the door and windows locked.

Spur let her come past him on the far side of the street. She turned and went down the steep hill that led to Charter Street. The horse and rig would make too much noise. He slid off the buggy seat and followed her, keeping her in sight, but not venturing too close.

She went straight down for three blocks, then over one block. As he paused behind a tree, he saw her go into the second of a row of five nearly identical gray houses. Lights were already on inside. He moved up as close as he could and noticed a new light glowing in the back room. There were two windows on his side of the house but both were carefully curtained, and the blinds had been drawn.

He gambled she would be in the house for some time. He checked in back and at the side. In the alley he found a rig that looked surprisingly like the one she had driven to the sailing ship that afternoon. She might be stopping here and moving on.

Spur turned and ran quietly back up the hill, panting at the exertion. He got in his rig and brought it to a stop at the end of the alley where her rig would emerge if it didn't turn around. Again he waited.

An hour later, just at 11:15, a horse and rider came out of the alley. It was a tall, sturdy horse, and the man who rode it was equally as tall. Spur figured the man was over six feet eight inches and maybe two hundred and eighty pounds. A lot of man, a lot of horse. He wore a hat that came down over his features.

Fifteen minutes later, he heard harness jangling, and the buggy in the alley came out. Spur crouched down in his rig so as not to be seen. The other buggy turned to the left in the same direction that Spur was headed. He followed a block behind, and after three blocks thought he was onto something. He could not see who was in the rig, but chances were that it was Katherine Sanford. Where the hell was she going?

Ahead Spur saw the big man on the horse pass the buggy and ride his way. The man turned around and followed the rig almost a block behind.

Spur scowled. Was this big man following her? Or was he protection? He found out a block later when the big man wheeled his horse and charged straight at Spur's buggy. Only by turning aside quickly could Spur avoid a collision. Twice more the large rider and his huge black horse charged Spur's carriage and twice more Spur had to pull sharply to the side to miss him.

As quickly as he attacked, the man was gone.

Spur looked ahead but could find no evidence of the other buggy.

He raced down one street after another looking, but he could not find the rig anywhere. He had been challenged and detained and thrown off the scent.

Spur took the next logical step. He continued in the direction he had been going and half a mile later he jogged over one block to the first prime suspect foundry. This one had all the needed equipment, and it was small enough. He found a watchman near the front gate and stopped.

"Good evening, sir. Are you the watchman here?"

" 'Pears as how, young feller."

"Been with the company long?"

"Ten year if it's been a day."

"Good. Notice anything unusual tonight?"

"How unusual?" the watchman said and sent a squirt of tobacco juice into the dust a foot from Spur's boots.

"Any people trying to break in, trying to use any of the machinery."

"Hail, why would they want to do that? They got to work here all day. You want them to come back at night, too?"

"No, not the regular workers, strangers."

"Hail, no. Nobody wants to get in there. I just walk around and scoot the kids away now and again."

"You sure, nothing unusual has been happening around here tonight?"

"Damn sure. Now I got to make my rounds. Promised Mr. Nelson I'd do that every hour on the hour, and sure looks like it's coming up on just after midnight."

"Right, yes, you do that." Spur waved at the watchman as he went back through the main gate and locked it. McCoy looked around. A stamping press striking off the coins would make considerable noise. This was a business and light industry area, no houses, no small shops with owners living over them. Might not be a soul within a mile.

That, along with the press being in a sturdy building which would muffle sound, were two big reasons this could be one of the Foundries used by the counterfeiters. He would check the other. If it was as dark and dead as this one, he might slip back here for an unannounced look around.

Spur stepped into his buggy and drove away.

On the other side of the board fence, Hop Choy watched through a crack between the boards as Spur talked to the guard. Hop had his pistol out and hammer back. He decided he would shoot the stranger and not simply warn the others. This was the same man in the buggy he had seen before.

The big man knew he should warn Miss Sanford, but he did not know how. He had never learned to read or write. His tongue had been gone for twenty years. He watched in satisfaction as the stranger drove away. It was safe after all. There was no reason to tell Miss Sanford that he had seen the man following her from the small gray house. Everything would be all right. Miss Sanford told him that she would take care of him. She promised he would be safe and would not have to go back to China. He liked it here. He had a house of his very own! Yes he shared it with Miss Sanford sometimes, but she told him it was his for as long as he wanted it.

Hop Choy smiled as he let the hammer down gently on the round in the chamber and put the six-gun in his holster. He would walk his rounds again. He had to protect Miss Sanford.

Spur McCoy drove to the second foundry. It was smaller, and he soon found out it had no night watchman. He jumped over the fence from the step of his buggy and toured the plant. There was no lights on anywhere, no one hiding in the shadows, and no one was trying to counterfeit coins. The foundry was uninvolved, at least for now. So where had Katherine Sanford gone? And why had the big man on the large horse made sure that Spur could not follow her?

He drove back to the small gray house and watched it for an hour. There was no movement in or out. He waited another half hour by his pocket watch, then drove away.

McCoy had tried to reason it out. Katherine was up to something. Fact: she had in her possession counterfeit coins. One had surfaced at the bank and the second time there were at least a dozen of them. Fact: she had gone in disguise somewhere. Fact: she had an accomplice who shielded her, and prevented Spur from following her.

Speculation: right now Katherine and some helpers could be striking off counterfeit gold double eagles.

Fact: he had not walked around the Nelson foundry and metal plant. He had taken the watchman's word for it. Why couldn't the watchman have been one of them, sharing in the proceeds? It might not have been the real watchman at all.

Spur turned his rig toward the Nelson foundry. He would come up quietly from the back. He would listen and watch. They would need lights, and he imagined that there would be considerable sound.

He parked the rig a block away from the back of the large yard and moved up silently.

Lights! He could see lights in on one of the buildings near the center of the complex. The board fence in back had been put up as a boundary marker more than a barrier. He went over it easily and crouched in the darkness. He heard a hiss of steam and a metalic clang somewhere ahead. Was that how it sounded like when a coin was struck? He wasn't sure.

Spur moved forward, misjudged a step and kicked a square of sheet metal, tipping it over and slamming a loud foreign sound through the back yard.

He bent low and waited, but neither saw nor heard anything unusual. Hoping that no one heard the noise, Spur moved forward again toward the lights and the sound. He came to a large building that was dark and edged around it. The next one was his target. But the building where he had seen lights was silent and dark. It must have been the following one. He hurried around the side of the dark structure and checked the next two buildings. Both were also dark.

Spur stood and rubbed his jaw. He had seen lights. He knew that. Had someone heard him coming and blown out the lamps? He could get the guard and demand to investigate the whole area. But that could be difficult, since he had no real authority here, no warrant to search.

Only suspicion.

He waited and watched.

After five minutes he had heard nothing. The only light he could see was a small lantern in the shack beside the main gate where the watchman sat. He could have been mistaken about the lights. The sound was better evidence. He would come back tomorrow and talk to the owner again, perhaps inspect the area.

Spur made his way to the back of the lot, climbed over the fence and drove away. A half mile down the street, he turned and came back past the plant. It was quiet and dark, just the way he had left it before. Perhaps tonight wasn't the night. But he became more convinced that this was the place where the counterfeiting was being done.

All he had to do was catch them at it.

He drove back to the hotel, parked his rig in back and went up to one of his four rooms he hadn't used, 319. Spur pulled his boots off and his jacket and pants, then fell on the bed and tried to relax. But his mind kept churning. Tomorrow he would go see Juan Pico. The Mexican had offered help and now he would take it. He wanted a dusk to daylight watch kept on that foundry. He wanted to get the description of anyone passing a counterfeit double eagle. And he was going to find out who owned that small gray house. The county clerk would be able to tell him. Then Spur slept.

CHAPTER TWELVE

It was 10 A.M. before Spur awoke the next morning. He seldom slept in that late. He shaved carefully, put on his conservative brown suit and sent his other two out to be cleaned. Then he had a quick breakfast and took a cab to the San Francisco county building and found the county clerk. It took them ten minutes to find the legal description of the property from the address. The ledger provided the tax paying owner.

"Legal owner of that plot is Katherine L. Sanford, and one Hop Choy, Chinese, I would imagine. They are listed as co-owners." As the clerk with a green eyeshade said it he shook his head. "Now why would a rich lady like her want a dumpy little place like that?"

"Maybe she has two or three thousand little

houses like that one," Spur said. He thanked the clerk and left knowing that things were looking worse for sweet little Katherine. Her troubles were not only sexual, that was growing plainer all the time.

He drove to a point where he could see the front door of the small gray house and waited. It was his major connection to the counterfeiters. He was sure now that they used the house as a headquarters, or at least Katherine did. She must have more men than the giant. But he had seen no others at the house. Surely she couldn't do it all by herself.

Spur had a quick lunch at a nearby café and watched the front door again. Within a half hour the big man came out and Spur now saw that he was Chinese. He had to be Hop Choy. In the daylight Spur increased his estimate of the man's size: He would go six feet eight and three hundred pounds. Not a man to tangle with. Hop Choy turned at the sidewalk and started off downtown. Spur tied the reins on his rig and followed.

Ten minutes later they were still walking. Spur had brought his gun and gunbelt along and had put half a box of loose shells in his jacket pocket just in case.

They passed through the busy shops and stores going toward a section that residents had long since dubbed *China Town* because of its high percentage of Chinese residents. Hop Choy worked his way through a crowd, avoided a small prancing dragon made of paper and animated by half a dozen children. He vanished into a store that seemed to cater to non-Chinese customers.

Spur walked in and stayed to one side as the man bought several items, paid for them with a double gold eagle, and then left with his change. Spur wanted to run up and test the coin, but there wasn't time. Already the mountain of a man had left.

Spur hurried out and spotted Hop Choy's head and shoulders over the shorter Chinese as he went down the street passing the time window shopping. He bought nothing else, but looked at various Chinese items offered for sale.

For a moment the man turned back and Spur was worried about getting too close. Then he realized Hop Choy would not know him. He had never seen Spur's face close enough to recognize him.

But he did. Hop Choy looked directly at Spur a moment later and he growled and pushed aside two small Chinese women and rushed toward Spur. The Secret Agent saw him coming. His back was at a plate glass window of a store, and a dozen children and woman surrounded him. There was no place to run.

He pulled the .44 and shouted.

"Hop Choy! Stay there. Stop!" He kept coming. Spur lifted the .44 and blasted a shot into the air. Hop Choy looked up and snorted, charging the last ten feet toward Spur. It was a beautiful and dramatic way to get a tracker off your trail, Spur thought in the few seconds before the Chinese mountain landed in his face.

Hop Choy didn't hesitate. He dove straight for Spur, his big hands out. Spur waited until the last critical split second, then he pivoted away as Spanish bullfighters did and brought the side of the .44

pistol down hard on the back of his attacker's neck. Hop Choy pawed at the empty air where McCoy had been, then felt the blow on his neck and dropped to his knees. He turned growling, making angry non-words in his throat as he started to get up. Spur powered another stroke with the .44 along Hop Choy's head and the huge man grunted, his arms dropped and he sank slowly in the street, his head a foot from a string of Chinese firecrackers.

Excited words in Chinese came from every side. Spur realized he was a stranger in a foreign land. He held the pistol up and waved his free hand for people to get out of his way. By then the street was full. Curious Chinese hurried up to see the fight.

The people were parting for him. Some seemed to be just off the boat in their coolie hats and Chinese robes. Others were smartly dressed Americanized businessmen. Many wore old clothes, and he saw more than one with the bleary eyes of the opium pipe.

Another half block and he would be out of the mess and free to turn down a street that led out of China Town. But Spur did not make it to that corner.

Three large men over six feet tall, thickly built and each carrying a two foot long Chinese sword, suddenly blocked his path. Two had angry scars on their cheeks. The third had a half healed slash across one arm and another on his bare torso.

All three were bare to the waist. They wore red bands around their heads and he heard someone behind him whisper to someone. The words were "Kwong Dock Tong."

Spur steadied himself. Tong. The strong, vicious, ruling gang that had usurped regular policing in China Town, and had taken it over much the way Juan Pico controlled his sector. Only here there were competing tongs. Spur knew that the Kwong Dock group was the first of the Mainland China societies to be transferred to America. It was the strongest, and it looked like these three enforcers were unhappy with him.

One of the trio edged around Spur and ran to Hop Choy who still lay in the street. The other two advanced slowly, moved six feet apart and came toward him.

Spur waited for them. He calmly thumbed a round into his six-gun to replace the fired bullets, and put a sixth in the empty chamber where usually the hammer rested. He would need six shots to get out of this he was certain.

McCoy called up his best parade ground voice and bellowed at the two Tong enforcers in front of him, shouting with such derision that they didn't have to understand the language to get the idea.

"You sorry looking women's helpers! You couldn't whip a house full of little boys and old women! Your sisters could knock you down with one backhanded slap!"

The first tong man roared in anger and charged forward swinging the sharp blade like a scythe. Spur fired twice, both rounds jolted into the Chinese's right leg, one .44 round broke the smaller leg bone and the enforcer crashed to the street and rolled over twice before he dropped his sticker and screamed as he grabbed his broken leg.

The second Chinese pulled two four-inch throwing knives from his belt and showed one to Spur. He laughed and came forward.

Police whistles down the street slowed, then stopped the big Chinese. He turned and stared toward the whistles. As he did Spur sprinted into the first shop behind him, ran through it to the back where he found another building filled with Chinese women working at some kind of craft. He hurried on through into the alley.

A dozen children looked up, screeched in terror at seeing a white man in their play yard. They watched silently as he ran down the street. The man who had gone to see Hop Choy appeared in the alley in front of Spur, cutting off his escape.

Spur turned to a door, kicked it open and rushed inside. He saw only a dimly lit room and a surprised Chinese woman who stared at him as he ran past.

The corridor narrowed, then went down, and he knew he should turn back, but there was no chance with the tong man following up behind him. The passage became smaller, and then the floor turned to dirt and the walls became raw wood. The roof was held up with mining type square set timbers. The only lights were torches placed at ten feet intervals. The smoke was heavy. He ran on. Ahead he saw a light, and soon the dirt floor gave way to planks, and the walls were covered. The route slanted upward slightly. Spur came to another corridor that opened into a long, low ceilinged room filled with pallets. On each small bed lay a man. Here and there lay a woman. All were smoking the long tubed pipe, and the sweet smell of opium smoke filled the chamber.

Glazed eyes turned to watch him. No one moved more than eyes as he ran to the far side where he entered a higher priced den, with bunks and tables. There was also a slender, naked Chinese girl giving comfort to the customers and always there was the long stemmed pipe and the tubes and the water jars.

Someone shouted at him in Chinese and he ran ahead. Now the hallway had doors on both sides. An occasional scream stabbed through the dimly lit rooms as Spur kept moving. The level dropped again and he descended a steep slope into a sunlit room where three naked men sat on cushions watching six nude Chinese girls dancing.

Two men shouted at Spur who hurried on into a closed room where a small Chinese woman nodded at him and waved to him to follow her. He noticed various pictures on the walls, all Oriental pornographic art. Each depicted a different method of intercourse.

The small woman led him into a room to one side and turned. She was holding a small caliber pistol in her hand. She smiled and took the revolver from his holster. There was no chance to knock away her weapon or beat her to the draw. She was crafty and wise in the way of guns. When she had his weapon, she lifted her gun and smiled.

"Now, crazy American, how do you want to die?"

Spur watched her closely. She was serious. He held his wounded arm as it throbbed again.

"American. No white man has ever been in this room before. None would dare to come here. Some of my small friends must have been chasing you."

"They are not small."

She laughed. As she did one of the tong enforcers burst into the room. He lifted his sword, but a curt command in Chinese stopped him. The two spoke softly for a moment, he angry and arguing, she with the tone and manner of authority. She looked at him. Then nodded and laughed. She said something to the man with the sticker and walked away.

The point of the sword touched Spur's side.

"Go," the Chinese commanded. Spur moved in the direction indicated. They went through another corridor, down some steps, up another flight and finally to a building where Spur thought he could hear people in the street.

They stopped at a door, and Spur found no chance to break away or to attack the big guard. Then his hands were tied behind his back and he was blindfolded while the big man held the sword at Spur's throat.

He was marched outside and helped into a buggy. After a short ride, Spur was taken out of the rig. He could smell the salt air. They were at the waterfront. A moment later a net dropped over him and he was pushed off his feet. He tried to yell as he was hoisted into the air upside down and swung to one side. He hit something, bounced off it and then was lowered with a bump as he fought the heavy net.

It came away quickly and hands caught him, carried him and then untied his hands. When they removed the blindfold Spur found himself below deck on an ocean going sailing ship. A big sailor with a patch over one eye waved a foot long knife at Spur and shouted at him in a foreign language. He pointed to a black hole.

Spur was shoved and pushed and jammed down the three foot square hole and dropped six feet to the hold below.

Shanghaied!

The tong had sold his body for three dollars, and unless he did something quickly, he would be on a year-long cruise to the South Pacific and perhaps Europe.

"Anyone else here?" Spur asked.

Someone laughed from the far corner. It was so dark Spur couldn't see his hands. Another voice came, half drunk, half frightened.

"Hell yes, six of us so far. Welcome aboard."

"Hear we're heading for the Philippines," another voice said.

"Not me," Spur said. "I'm heading back to the docks. Anything down here to use for a club? Feel around, anybody sitting on a board or a stick, part of a crate, anything?"

"Not me, mate. Clean as a baby's bottom."

"Nothing here."

Spur looked around. The hatch cover fit loosely and let in a little light. Now his eyes had adjusted and he could see the twenty foot square hold, and five other men sitting or lying on the deck. A ladder led up to the hatch cover. He crawled up and tried to lift it, but it was locked down.

He took stock. He still had the four inch knife in his boot they had not taken, and the .44 rounds in his belt and in his pocket.

"Anybody have a hide-out gun they missed?" Spur asked.

Again negative answers.

"What about a pair of pliers? Hell, that's too much to ask for." Spur checked the hatch cover again. There was a spot near the top where he could put in a charge and the force would be directed upward. Great. He dropped back to the bottom of the hold and sat down, took a small note pad from his pocket and ripped six pages from it.

"Anyone ever taken .44 rounds apart to get the black powder out?"

"Yeah, I did during the war," an older voice said.

"Come over here and help me," Spur said. "And just maybe all of us can get out of here. When are we supposed to sail?"

"With the midnight tide," the older voice said.

Spur took from his pocket twenty .44 rounds. He got his knife from his boot and began loosening up the lead slugs in the copper casings. The older man was a dark shadow, but he took one of the loosened rounds and twisted the lead out with his teeth.

"Yes!" Spur said. "That's the way. Now empty the powder on these sheets of paper. They'll have to do for containers."

They worked for almost ten minutes. Eventually Spur and the older man had emptied the twenty rounds from his pocket and the eighteen from his belt. They made a stack of six of the pages filled with powder.

"Any sailors here?" Spur asked.

"Yeah, I been over the line a few times," a voice from the far corner said.

"What's the procedure on deck? When will the least men be up there?"

"Most of the hands will be on shore leave today. Just a few to load, and then the rest will come back two hours before sailing."

"How many up there right now?" Spur asked.

"Five, maybe six."

Spur took off his three inch wide leather belt with the heavy silver buckle. He pivoted a four inch blade from the buckle and locked it in place so it extended three inches beyond the end of the buckle. He had shaved with it from time to time. By wrapping the end of the belt around his hand he was able to make a sharp and dangerous swinging type weapon.

"Now would be as good a time as any?" Spur asked.

"Yep, if you want to get your head bashed in. Nobody knows you're here. They got nothing to lose."

"I have plenty to lose by sailing," Spur said. "Any of you with me?"

Four were. Spur explained what they would do. He went up the ladder and placed the packages of black powder in the corner of the hatch cover and trailed a quarter inch wide line of powder a foot along the two-by-four from the small bomb as a fuse.

"Ready?" Spur asked below. They were. He took a sulphur stinker match from his pocket and lit it. When it blazed up fully he touched it to the powder trail and swung out and dropped to the bottom of the hold. He rolled to the far corner with the others as the black powder bomb went off.

It made twice the explosion Spur thought it would. As soon as it crashed, he was up and running for the ladder. The charge had splintered the hatch cover, blown half of it off and broken the wooden latch that held it down. Spur jammed the rest of it upward and jumped on deck just as a seaman came out of a forward cabin, a knife in one hand, a half eaten apple in the other. He yelled and charged, but Spur stood his ground. At the last moment, Spur swung the belt once around his head, then leaped forward and aimed the blade at the seaman's legs. It missed one but slashed a three inch wound in the other leg. Blood poured out and the seaman screamed as he fell to the deck. The other men had streamed out of the hold. Two ran and jumped into the water on the bay side, another charged a second sailor who had answered his friend's alarm. The man took a slash to the shoulder, but kicked the seaman in the groin and rushed for the gangplank.

Spur ran in the same direction. A large man lumbered into their path. Spur swung the belt, missed, swung it again and the blade slashed across the sailor's chest before he knew what he was fighting. He yelled and fell to one side. Spur and an older man from below ran down the gangplank, bowled over a small seaman who tried to stop them. They were free and ran along the dock and up the nearest street.

When they were two blocks away, Spur and the other man stepped into an alley and rested.

Spur held out his hand. "Spur McCoy," he said.

"Lenord Bruce, and I thank you. I had about given up. I'd been down there two days, and I don't think I could have survived a voyage on that wind-jammer."

"Where did they capture you?"

"A bar. I was drunk and broke. They sold me for four dollars."

"I was worth only three." Spur reached in his pocket, and found two gold double eagles, real ones. He gave them to the man and wished him luck, then hurried up the street where he could find a hack and get back to his hotel. A throbbing pain forced him to think about his shoulder. It was bleeding again. He'd have to go back to the doctor for a new bandage. He also wanted to see Juan Pico and talk about having that twelve-hour dusk to dawn watch on the three foundries. He was convinced that the gang was using one of them, probably Nelson's. All he had to do was catch them in the act. He would have the evidence any court would require for a quick conviction.

CHAPTER THIRTEEN

It was nearly four in the afternoon before Spur made it to Olivera Street to talk to Juan Pico. The Mexican leader received him at once.

"A watch on the foundries? Yes, I agree. A good plan. And if we see or hear any activity, my men will report it directly to you. Where? Your hotel room at the San Franciscan?"

"A message in my key box room 310 will do it. Could they start tonight?"

"It is now being arranged for a team of two men to be on guard at all three of the firms. That way one can report to you while the other observes."

"Thanks, Don Pico. I appreciate your help. The United States government appreciates your assistance as well. If this turns out the way it looks now, there should be enough money recovered so all of the counterfeits can be redeemed at face value by a local banker. They will have to be picked up, of course, but I don't think any of your people will lose a peso because of these bad coins."

"Good! *Bueno!* I am glad." He frowned. "I know it is not polite to ask but you seem a bit worse for the wear. Have you had any problems with my people?"

Spur touched a torn place on his jacket sleeve, a bruise on his cheek and the newly bandaged shoulder.

"Not at all, Don Pico. I enjoy coming to Olivera Street. It was China Town where I had my problems. I got involved in an underground maze and never did find my way out."

"You were in the *Palace of Pleasure?*"

"I'm not sure, but there were a lot of pleasures offered the paying customers."

"You are a lucky man to come out of there alive. Even most of the Chinese living here don't know where it is."

"It was not a memorable experience. I better get moving. Thanks again for your help."

Twenty minutes later Spur sat in the afternoon sunshine. He decided that another stretch of watching the small gray house might be productive. This time he chose the far end of the alley where he could see the house and the buggy that was usually tied up behind it. It appeared to be the same one Katherine had used before.

A little more than an hour after Spur took up his watch, a man rode in on a sorrel with a white mane and tail. He tied his mount to a fence and sat down in the shade and waited. He kept looking up the alley, away from Spur.

For a second Spur wondered if this man was watching the gray house as well. No other law enforcement people in town knew about the counterfeiting. Who could he be? Spur waited a half hour more and the sun was beginning to go down. A young boy came out of the back of the gray house and put something in the buggy. As he moved, Spur recognized the stride, the proud carriage. It was Katherine dressed as a boy again.

The watcher ahead of Spur turned away and became busy with some boxes in the alley. Obviously he didn't want to be recognized by Katherine. Spur watched the man in the late afternoon light. He was maybe five feet ten, red hair showed under a high crown range hat. He wore a six-gun tied low on his right leg.

If he were with the San Francisco police, they should compare notes. Spur left the buggy and walked down the alley toward the man, making just enough noise to make him aware that someone was coming. Spur's gunbelt was back in place, with a replacement .44 and belt rounds repositioned.

The man with the sorrel looked up quickly, stared at Spur for a moment, then mounted up fast.

"Hold it!" Spur shouted. But the redhead pulled the sorrel around and rode out past the gray house toward the street. Spur leaped in his buggy and slapped the reins on the horse's back as he tried to follow the man. He didn't have a chance of staying with the horseback rider, but he could get a general direction where he was headed.

Spur came around the mouth of the alley. The rider was half a block ahead. He turned left and headed for the bay side of the peninsula. Spur stayed with him. Soon the redhead had a full block lead, but he didn't try to lose Spur. Was he simply leading Spur on, working him into some kind of a trap?

Spur kept driving, saw the sorrel turn again toward the bay and ride down a street fronting the harbor where the fishing fleet tied up. There were a hundred fishing boats, none over thirty feet long. Most were identical, with one mast and no cabin. They were piled with nets. Some had outriggers for lines to be let down.

The man left his horse at the embarcadero and rushed to a pier and stepped on board a fishing boat. As Spur watched from the pier the man hurried from one boat tied along side another until he was half way across to the next pier. Spur couldn't figure out what he was trying to do.

Maybe he was working over to the second pier in order to get away. Spur left his rig and made his way to the next wooden structure jutting into the bay. As unobtrusively as possible he went past the fish sellers to the midpoint and watched the redhead's progress. He ducked into one fishing boat after another, coming out on the other side and stepped into the next boat tied alongside.

It had to be a tangled problem when all those boats started out for a day's fishing first thing in the morning, Spur decided. For a moment he lost the redhead. Then he spotted the man moving across the last three boats to the pier. Spur was between the man and the shore.

Someone behind Spur shouted. He looked back and saw two men rolling a fish box on wheels toward him. It was filled with silver, flopping fish. Spur leaped to one side but was too late. The fish box hit him, tipped over and a hundred pounds of wet, sticky fish flooded down on top of him on the pier. He saw the redhead run past. By the time Spur got to his feet, the man was almost to the street.

McCoy threw a fish at the fisherman who had dumped them on him and rushed after his quarry.

McCoy lost the redhead twice, picked up his trail in the sparsely peopled dock area, and at last caught him just before he slipped into a small seafood restaurant. He did not even try to draw his gun.

Spur grabbed his shirt front and pushed the man against the side of the building.

"I told you to stop back in the alley. Why did you run?" Spur asked.

"Thought you were trying to rob me."

"That won't work, try another reason."

"Look, I wasn't supposed to be in the alley. I figured you were working for her."

"Who?"

"The woman who lives in the gray house."

"Why were you spying on her?"

"She owes me money. I thought she was leaving town."

"Who is the lady who lives there?"

"Dorothy Jones."

"Never heard of her. Who is she?"

"Nobody you would know." He turned. "Why were you in the alley?"

"I'm the one asking the questions, and you've been lying to me. Now why were you watching the place?"

"She had been meeting someone there, and I had to know who it was. It was a lover."

"And you're her husband."

"Yes, of course."

"Wrong again. I know who owns that house. It isn't anybody named Dorothy Jones. When are you going to start telling me the truth?"

"I don't have to tell you a damned thing!" Then his shoulders slumped, his face turned sad almost to the point of tears, and he shook his head. "No, no. Maybe I should tell someone." He rubbed one hand across his face and Spur followed the motion.

Too late McCoy realized he had been fooled. The redhead's other hand flashed down, drew his pistol and waved it in Spur's face before he could draw.

"Now, back off you sonofabitch, or I'm gonna cut you down to size with a few lead slugs. You savvy? Lay down on the sidewalk, face to the boards. Right now!"

Spur could do nothing else. He went down, stretched out on the wooden sidewalk.

"You stay there for five minutes or I'll blast a hole a foot wide through your belly! You try following me and you're going to discover yourself dead and gone to hell!" The redhead glared at Spur, then ran down the block and around the corner.

Spur stood and let the man go. He wasn't San

rancisco police, and if he were one of the men working with Katherine, why would he be spying on her? Another piece to the puzzle. He had to get all of them put together, and the quicker the better.

It was a little after six when Spur returned to the San Franciscan Hotel, ordered up bath water and washed the last of the fish scales out of his hair. He would smell like fish for a week.

There had been two messages in his 310 box. One was from Juan Pico. It read:

The situation with the counterfeit double eagles is reaching critical proportions. My people took in twenty more of them during the past two days. These have come through my unofficial banking fuction for the smaller merchants. Something must be done at once.

If the situation is not cleared up in two days, I will put a ban on the use of the double eagle in my area. This could have startling effects on the rest of the business firms in San Francisco, and could lead to a collapse in public support for the gold standard in the city.

This is by no means a threat. Only to urge you on to greater efforts for everyone's benefit. My men are on post watching the three foundries. Any activity report will come directly to you.

Spur read the note again. He could watch the small gray house tonight or he could go see Katherine. His shoulder ached again and he changed his mind.

He read the second note. It was from Mrs. Engleton, the society matron with the sexy little black maid. She suggested they have a late dinner at her place. He smiled but shook his head. He wasn't strong enough for that kind of a workout yet.

Spur decided it was time for a real rest. He would have a good dinner downstairs and get to bed early for a long sleep.

That was when he remembered his appointment for tonight. He had to see one more artist to help keep his cover intact. He wasn't even sure who it was. Then he remembered. The artist who signed himself Radiji. Sounded like an East Indian. Spur would much rather have caught up on his sleep, but he had that 8 P.M. appointment. He would go. This would be his last artist contact. His cover wasn't going to be that important after the next two days.

Tomorrow he would see Katherine and try to trip her up about the gold eagles. It was either that or make a raid on the gray house. He had to know where they were doing the counterfeiting, and catch them in the act.

Spur left the hotel by the side door at ten minutes to eight and took a hack to the address. It was not the best section of town and in a two storey building. Artists always wanted a skylight.

He went up the steps to the second floor and knocked on the only door there. Nobody answered. He knocked again and at last someone came. When the door opened a short chunky woman stared at him, then she smiled.

"Oh, you're the buyer from New York, the important big man coming to bless us with his presence. Come on in. I know you won't buy nothing. You big shot fuckers never do, but come in anyway. Hell, what I got to lose?"

"I was looking for Radiji. Is this the right address?"

"Yeah, right, it is. I'm feeling bitchy tonight. Come on in. What do you want to drink?"

"Nothing, thanks. I wanted to see some of the work of this person called Radiji. Is he here?"

"Damn! You did it too. I am Radiji. Radiji ain't no goddamn man, she's me, I am Radiji!"

"Well, good. What a pleasant surprise. If you would sign your work Helen or Ruth, the whole world would know that you're a woman. Why hide behind one name?"

"I ain't hiding. Tried it the other way. Sold maybe five or six paintings a year, all to women. Started using Radiji and I sell enough to live on. Not well, as you can see, but I get the rent paid." She stared up at him. "You really want to look at my work, or you just here because you said you would come?"

"I want to look, otherwise I wouldn't be here. You may not believe it, but you're not the only one with problems."

"Yeah, all right, sorry. I guess I did get shouting there before I knew your feelings. Back this way."

She led him down a hall to a big studio with a skylight. The room was thirty feet long, and he saw that a wall had been torn out. Along one side there were canvases hung on the wall. All were of nude women.

"You knew I only did tit paintings. Tits and ass
that's what you men like on the wall and in the bed.
So that's what I paint. Not dirty pictures, artistic
ones. Beautiful women with a few or no clothes on.
Men buy them. Some women hate them. I make a
living. How many do you want me to send to New
York on the train?"

Spur moved a lamp and checked one two by three
foot horizontal picture. It was beautiful. A woman
lay on a velvet couch. She was well rounded, like a
Rubens, big breasted and painted in an artistic
pose that could be thought of as sexy. Her crotch
was delicately covered with a trailing hand, but her
breasts thrust up and out invitingly.

"You do good work."

"Hell, I know that, not great, but good. That's
why I'll sell wholesale, no consignment. Sell outright
a dozen, twenty, two dozen. And I'll give you a fifty
percent cut in my retail price. Means you can double
your money fast."

It was true. Spur had seen paintings of less quality
in some New York galleries at three times the price
she asked. He suddenly wished he were a real art
buyer.

They moved the lamps so he could see the rest of
her work. Every piece was good. The faces were as
marvelously done as the nude bodies.

He asked her prices.

"You want a dozen, they are eighty dollars each.
You want twice that you can have them for sixty-five
dollars. Any of these tit paintings will sell in New
York for a hundred and fifty. I used to work there, I
know."

"You're right. I just don't have that kind of money left in my budget. I wish I had stopped here earlier on my trip."

The woman nodded. "Shit! That's happened to me the last two times. I don't sell on the street. I'd be busted."

"How much do you get for one painting?"

"That bitch there with the pink tits is sixty-five on the street. I haggle down to about forty. You want her she's wrapped up for you for twenty bucks. You can do me some good back east."

Spur pulled out a good double eagle from his pocket and handed it to her. "Sold."

"Hot damn!" She grinned. "You want the bonus that goes along with the picture?"

"What's that?"

"Surprise. You come over here while I wrap up the picture. Can't let you carry Polly there around the street all naked."

She led Spur into an adjoining room. It was small and had a couch, chair and a mirror.

"This is a model's dressing room. I'll be right back. You wait here."

She left and a minute later the opposite door opened and a young girl no more than thirteen came in. She wore only a chemise that barely covered her crotch. Her young, small breasts made only dimples in the chemise.

Spur frowned. "Sorry, I must be in the wrong place."

"No, this is the right place." She turned around slowly. "Do you like me? My name is Willa."

Spur was slowly beginning to understand. She

pulled the chemise off and stood nude before him. Her breasts were just beginning to swell. Only a soft brown hint of crotch hair showed.

"You like Willa better this way?"

"No, Willa, put the chemise on." Spur turned to the door. Radiji came in carrying the wrapped picture in front of her. When she put it down she was naked as well.

"Well, you've met Willa. She and me, we're the bonus. You can bang away on either one of us, or both. That's the fucking bonus you get for buying a picture."

Spur grinned at Radiji. She was pleasingly and frankly fat. Her large breasts sagged halfway to her belly, which bulged over her crotch so no pubic hair showed. Her arms and legs were chunky as well.

Spur waved at the girl. "Get her out of here."

Radiji nodded and the girl went out the door. Her expression hadn't changed the whole time she was in the room.

"You'll get in trouble offering that young girl," Spur said.

"Haven't yet. She's my daughter."

"That's worse yet."

"Ease up, McCoy. Ease up and relax and enjoy a good fuck. You got a pecker in them pants of yours or not?"

Spur watched the fat woman moving in front of him, doing a little bump and grind, waggling her huge, sagging breasts.

"Hey, I give a nice, soft, easy cushion of a ride." She knelt in front of Spur and pulled open his fly, dug inside until she found his hardness and yelped in success.

"Damn, he's small, but I found him. He grow any bigger?"

Spur laughed and let down his pants and drawers and followed her to the couch.

She flopped down on her back and spread her legs.

"Want me to pee a little to give you a target?" she said and wailed in laughter.

While she was laughing Spur dropped between her legs and jolted inside her ending the laugh with a gasp of pleasure. Then she looked up and frowned.

"Someday women is gonna be appreciated, you know that? We'll get the vote and be equal in the law. Now men think of us as tits and cunt, that's it. They ball us and expect us to raise the kids and feed everybody and spread our legs and open our cunts to them whenever they bellow. Hell, that's partly why I left my old man. He kept demanding. I told him to stuff it up his own ass for a change. Came out here. So I fuck when I want to, why not? Men sure as hell do. Why can't I? I want to let a man have a go at me, that's my own fucking business." She laughed at her own pun.

"Christ, you got a cock like a big oak tree, you know that? I ain't been touched in deep that way in years. Oh, god! That is pure wild. Usually I don't come at all, no fucking climax. Sometimes I pretend, but this time for damn sure I feel it building up. Oh, yeah!"

Spur concentrated on jolting into her so he scraped past her tender clit, and each time she worked her own passion higher and higher.

Before Spur reached his climax, the chunky woman screeched in pain and delight. She rattled and shook like a cattle car on the railroad. She roared and bellowed her delight and soon she was panting and wailing as if she had never been here before.

Her performance jolted Spur into action and his climax kept hers alive. She worked through the whole gambit of her joy ride again, screaming at the end, then nearly fainting.

Spur slid away from her and watched her recuperate. Her breath came in ragged gasping surges. Sweat beaded her forehead and ran in a little stream down between her breasts. She moaned softly and reached for him.

"Don't go. Once more. Give Willa a ride like that. Show her how good it can be."

Spur hadn't even taken off his pants. Now he pulled up his clothes and shook his head at the chunky woman sprawled on the couch.

"I told you. I don't touch anybody that young. Forget it."

She sat up and he grinned at the way her breasts swung around.

"You got too damn many principles."

"Probably, but that's just the way I am. You got your bonus, I got my bonus. We'll leave Willa out of it." Spur paused. "I'm going to try to rustle up some demand for your work. I'll be in St. Louis soon, and

I should be able to get an order for you there. Keep watching your mail." Spur left her on the couch and went into the front room.

Willa sat there, still in the chemise. She was looking at a magazine. She smiled at him.

"Thanks. I really don't like to do it."

"That's natural. You shouldn't yet. Tell your mother. Maybe she'll listen."

"Doubt it, but I'll try." She blushed. "Mr. McCoy, could I ask you something?"

He stopped. "Sure."

"Could I kiss you on the cheek? I'd really like that."

"So would I, Willa."

She jumped up and kissed him and stepped back. She smiled and ran toward the inside door. "I better get some clothes on, somebody might come in."

Spur McCoy picked up the painting which he planned to ship to St. Louis. It would hang over his bed. Fleurette would either love it or slash it to pieces. It would be interesting to see which one.

He went down to the street and walked back to the hotel. Now he could work on that good night's sleep.

CHAPTER FOURTEEN

As Spur was catching up on his sleep, Katherine Sanford held a special meeting of her gang. She loved to call them a gang, and made it clear to them that she was the leader, and that Burke was second in command.

They met in a small back room of a bar and gaming house near the outskirts of town, well away from any place that Spur McCoy might be seen. She waited until the bar wench had delivered warm beer to everyone, and a glass of white wine for her, then she grabbed their attention.

"We may have to kill someone," she said. She watched the reaction of each man. Tim Hackett, the die and metal expert, turned slightly pale and had a long pull on his beer. Burke Foster grinned and drew his six-gun and slid it back in leather three times. Hop Choy touched the bandage at the side of his face and nodded solemnly, anger, hatred in his usually calm eyes. Breed's face showed no change whatsoever, his black eyes flicked up to her face to see if she were serious, then he looked back at the table and nursed his beer.

"Anyone we know?" Burke asked.

"That's what I want to find out. Hop Choy has indicated that a tall white man hit him with a pistol. He does not know when the white man started following him, but, if I am right in interpreting what he tells me with sign language, he was the same fellow who was nosing around Nelson's the other night. The same man who talked to the night watchman."

"Christ, that is big trouble," Burke said. "Does he know about the gray house?"

"I don't know," Katherine said. "Have any of you seen him around there watching the place? Have you seen a tall man with sandy hair and a moustache in the alley or down the block, just sitting around, waiting, maybe watching?"

"Christ, that would be bad," Burke said. "If this guy knows about the gray house! Maybe we shouldn't use it for a while. Didn't you say we were about coming to the end of our string on this one, anyway? Maybe we should close it down now and take what we have and split it up the way we talked."

"No, it isn't that drastic. I know this man. His name is Spur McCoy. He says he's an art buyer from New York, but I don't believe him. I saw him one night with my banker, the banker who asked me about the counterfeit I let slip into a deposit I made."

"Maybe he's government," Hackett said. "They have one bunch of guys that worry about counterfeiting. Yeah, I think it's time we split the coins the way you said and go different directions."

"Stop it!" Katherine said. She hadn't changed clothes, and wore a dress that she realized now was too tightly revealing. Burke was drooling. "Just relax, everyone. When it's time to quit, I'll tell you all and everyone will be free and safe. This money is going to be no good if we're all in prison. So let me handle that end of it. All I want to know is if any of you have seen this Spur McCoy."

She looked at each of them again.

"Hell, we might have," Burke said. "I don't imagine you got a tintype of him so we could be sure."

She shook her head.

Burke shrugged. "Hell, I'll keep my eyeballs peeled." But inside Burke was worried. Her description fit the *hombre* in the alley who chased him down to the docks. He said he knew who lived in the gray house. If he knew and he suspected, then this McCoy could close in anytime. Burke had to get into motion. He had to get the coins out of the gray house. No big job, simply shoot the Chink and take the goods about two A.M. Easy. He would bring Breed along for protection, then give him a lead sandwich out the trail a ways. It had to be tonight. Things were closing in too damn fast. There was no chance that he was going to admit to Kate that he had seen McCoy and that McCoy knew about the gray house. If he did that, then he would have to explain to the damn black widow lady just what he was doing spying on the little gray house. He could not risk it if he wanted a shot at that treasure chest under the floor in the back bedroom. Best to dummy up and wait.

"I was hoping that some of you men had seen him hanging around. Even without that, it is now decision time. Tomorrow I'll be going on a little picnic with Mr. McCoy. I want Breed to follow us out of town and take care of him. Breed, I don't care how you do it, but don't get me all messed up. Understand? I don't want him falling on me or anything."

"Do a head shot, Breed," Burke suggested.

"I don't want to know the details. You better not follow us out. We'll go to Moon Rocks Bay, just south of town. You be there and take care of it. Then we won't have to worry about anything and we can finish five more strikings."

"Five?" Burke asked. "Thought you said two more the last time we were at Nelson's."

"Yes, but we can strike off four thousand dollars a night. I think we all could use just a little bit more cash when we split it."

Around the room heads nodded.

"Using that as a vote, we'll take care of Mr. McCoy and then have five more strikings. Now, that's all we need to settle. It's nice talking to you rich men, but I have to get back to a damn meeting about the opera."

166

Katherine went to the meeting, then to bed so she could get up early. She sent a note to Spur's hotel room inviting him to a picnic lunch, expounding on the beauty and seclusion of this place just out of town south. She told him to be at her door by eleven the next morning.

The following morning, Katherine was pleased to hear Spur arriving ten minutes early. She looked in the mirror one last time, pulled on her dress to show more cleavage, then went downstairs to give Spur a loving kiss and a promise of more to come.

"Mr. McCoy! It's so good to see you. I'm glad you can come on the picnic. The basket is all packed, and we have plenty of wine this time so we don't run out. It's in the carriage and I'll even let you drive."

She held her cheek out to be kissed and Spur brushed his lips against it. Then he turned her face and kissed her lips.

"Now that is better," Spur said. "I was hoping I could see you today. It's almost time for me to move on to Los Angeles. They are developing some very fine young artists down there, and some of the Mexicans are producing again."

"Oh, so soon? Then we shall make this a special time, an extra special, personal time for just the two of us. Darling, I almost can't wait!"

"Then let's get moving and see this idyllic glen you have found on the coast."

It took them an hour to drive there, and they reached it after going through a gate on a private road, then turning off and working up the coast a half mile. It was beautiful; one of those miniature coves less than fifty feet wide, with a sandy beach and rocks all the way around it and the surf crashing on the rocks and then sliding into the cove that was blue-water deep and calm.

Behind the beach lay a dense stand of young live oak and cotton woods. They walked the last two hundred yards where they spread the blanket out in the grass at the edge of the sand in the shade.

"Let's swim first," she said, and they raced each other to take off clothes. He stopped and watched her pull off her garments, throwing them on the grass. When her breasts burst into view he clapped and cheered. But she was off, running for the clear, cool waters.

Spur raced right after her. They both came up gasping for air and his arms went around her and they kissed and sank below the water laughing as they surfaced.

They stood in waist deep water and she kissed him hard, her tongue boring into his mouth, her hands playing with his growing erection. When the kiss ended, she yelped in delight.

"You did it! You're hard underwater. Oh, do it now, put it inside me when we're both underwater. I don't know if it can be done or not."

She wouldn't let him go and pulled at him. Spur shrugged, lifted her and positioned himself. With one stabbing thrust he penetrated her shrunken nether lips and she screeched in real pain. Then she burst out laughing.

"My god! It can be done. Just don't lay me down

on my back out here or we'll both drown."

She began moving back and forth, then forward and back as she built his passion and too soon he exploded inside her and sagged under water, rolling away as he came out of her. He swam twenty yards underwater to shore until he hit the sand, then he was up and running for the picnic basket.

"I'm starved, let's eat," he called. Spur used the few moments for a quick security check. He had not seen anyone when they drove in. There was a small farm or camp to the south, but they had turned north and there didn't seem to be anyone within two miles. Still he had a strange feeling, a hunch. Why was she so set on coming out here for a picnic? Spur was thinking of her more as a suspect than a casual friend and lover.

She came running up, her magnificent breasts swaying and bouncing and still dripping salt water. She sat on his lap and demanded that he kiss her all over. He started but never got past her breasts.

"You are so good!" she said. "We will make love ten times today, and you will be great. I have ways to help you. Now, the lunch."

They sat on the blanket, one on each side of the basket, and began the picnic. There was fried chicken, potato salad, fresh fruit, a half a dead-ripe watermelon, bottles of beer and wine, and cheese and a dozen different kinds of crackers.

She showed him some thin sandwiches made of crushed small shrimp and mixed with a little thick cream and chopped onions. It was delicious. He ate four. Once he saw her looking into the woods, and he wondered why. She might have heard someone.

"Are you nervous? Do we need to dress?" He asked her.

She shook her head. "Cover up that beautiful body? I won't let you. No, there is not a soul around for five miles. That's why I like it out here. We can go bare all day if we don't get sunburned. It is a marvelous fling."

She opened the wine and poured him a glass, then took a drink from the bottle before pouring her glass. "I get ahead that way." She stood and rubbed her breasts into his face and he caught one and chewed and she crooned.

Fifty yards away in the deep woods, Breed lay in his protective covering, not making a sound. A .50 caliber Sharps rifle lay beside him and his hand pumped up and down over his crotch.

"Damn, oh, damn! Oh, damn!" he whispered as he ejaculated into the hundred year old mulch of decomposed leaf mold under the trees. He wiped sweat off his forehead and picked up the Sharps.

She was so beautiful! Twice he had been ready to shoot, and then she moved or waved her bare ass in his direction or her big tits, and he put down the rifle and grabbed his stiff penis for one more masturbation.

Now he had to do it. They had been there an hour. He wanted to kill McCoy and then run up and throw her onto the blanket and demand sexual compensation. She would give it to him. She had loved his work a few nights ago.

Breed picked up the Sharps, made sure that it was

loaded and ready, then sighted in on the broad back of Spur McCoy. He would put a round through his spinal column, a much better target than a head. Sweat misted his eyes and he slashed it away.

Katherine stood and rubbed her breasts over the naked man, then lowered one breast into his mouth.

"Oh, damn, no!" Breed croaked. He pushed the Sharps to one side and a stick caught in the trigger. He pushed it again as he reached for his phallus. The pressure of the stick was more than the trigger could withstand; the trigger pushed, the hammer fell and the Sharps round exploded and screamed six feet over Spur's head.

McCoy dove away from the naked woman toward his clothes. He dragged his gunbelt off the top of his clothes and sprinted fifteen yards toward a sturdy live oak that would shield him.

Breed swore, jammed a new round into the Sharps and looked for his target. Katherine remained on the blanket. He checked the rest of the beach and the grass, then looked at the trees. For a moment the thrill of a fight settled over him. He realized that in the thick trees and brush a man with a six-gun would have the advantage. It was not a long range duel.

Spur checked his loads in the .44, then peered out from low on the oak, searching for the source of the rifle shot. He did not think it had been a warning. The elements were too perfect: it was a bushwhack killing. Only something had gone wrong. The report had been from a heavy rifle, a Spencer or a Sharps. If the gunman had been over thirty to forty yards away he had been a fool. How could he miss at that range?

Spur had thought it through. He called to Katherine.

"Take your clothes and get back to the buggy. Drive for town if you can. I'll hold this hardcase off whoever he is. Just go. Leave my clothes, but take yours. Now move before he fires again."

As soon as Spur shouted the commands, he dropped to his knees and crawled from his tree to another one to his left. The sound of the shot had come from that direction. It was the sort of sound placement he had learned to recognize and remember. It helped a person to stay alive.

Now he stood behind another big live oak and listened.

Nothing.

He detected movement ahead and to the left. Only a whisper. He knew Indians who couldn't move through dry woodlands that quietly. More soft sounds to the left. Retreating. The bushwhacker was moving out. Spur watched through the trees, but could see no sign of anyone. He ran lightly from tree to tree, working quickly out of the acre sized woods. As he remembered there was grasslands all around the spot of trees. Once to the edge of the oaks the ambusher would have no cover. The grass was waist high, but not heavy enough for a man to crawl through undetected.

Five minutes later Spur was at the edge of the woods. He stayed behind a big oak and scanned the area ahead. For a moment he saw movement a hundred feet ahead, then it blended back into the shadows.

The man was down there, worried about his next step. A horse? There should be a horse nearby. Spur sniffed the off shore breeze but could not detect any horse smells. Too much to hope for.

He waited.

Spur remembered a time in Arizona when he had outwaited an Indian lying half covered with sand in the desert. After two hours the Indian had moved an arm, and Spur shot him. He hoped this would not entail that much patience.

To the right he heard harness jangle and the sound of the horse moving the buggy. At least Katherine was away with no harm done. Now it was his turn to even the score with this bushwhacker.

Spur dodged around his tree and bolted fifteen yards to the next big oak to his left. It provided cover for him after ten steps and then he was behind it, panting, trying to hold his breath to listen.

No sounds.

Spur waited for five minutes.

A startled pheasant flew up from the grass twenty yards from the trees. Spur watched the spot with interest. Pheasants will let you walk within a foot of them and not move, blending in with the grass and shrubs. If one moved. . . .

Spur watched the flushing spot with intensity, and saw a wand of grass jiggle, then bend to the left, away from the woods.

His bushwhacker was moving through the grass. He was out of sight, which also meant he couldn't see out. Spur crouched and watched the gently swaying grass where he figured the killer had to be. He ran softly through the grass paralleling the bushwhacker. Soon he was ahead of him with an off shore wind blowing in his face. The waist high grass was tinder dry from the Santa Ana dry winds. Spur ran another twenty yards ahead of the crawler and cut at right angles to his former path until he estimated he was directly in front of the bushwhacker.

Spur brought a small packet of stinker matches from his pocket, broke off one and bent low, striking it on the bottom of the pack and touching off the dry grass. Flames leaped at the grass and Spur knelt there upwind, watching the breeze fan the flames.

It crackled, then the wind raced the flames through the grass as fast as a man could walk. Spur watched ahead, his .44 up and held with both hands. He heard a startled cry, then a figure leaped upright twenty feet in front of him and only a half dozen feet from the flames. Black smoke billowed toward him and he stared at it a moment.

That was when Spur fired. His round caught Breed in the left shoulder and knocked him down. He screamed as the fire raced toward him. Frantically he jumped up, holding his left shoulder, the rifle forgotten. He ran to the left to go around the end of the fire. Spur fired twice, aiming low into the grass hoping to hit his legs.

The first round missed, but the second sent Breed tumbling into the grass. He screamed in terror and hopped on one leg as he frantically worked around the far end of the fire.

Spur figured the grass would burn itself out when it came to the live oaks where it would have little grass to continue. He would worry about that later. He ran hard now around the end of the blackened grass until he found Breed lying on his back, breathing heavily of the sweet non-smoky air.

Breed looked up at Spur and spat at him. Spur lowered the muzzle of the .44.

"Indian, aren't you? Who paid you to kill me?"

The man didn't reply.

Spur shot him in the other leg. Blood gushed out as the Indian screamed.

"Who paid you to kill me?"

"I won't tell you."

"You don't understand. I don't like people to shoot at me. It makes me unhappy with whoever does it and whoever hires him to do it. I plan on seeing justice done on both counts."

Spur shot Breed in the right arm. More blood surged.

Breed screamed again.

"I understand this is remote and isolated. No one ever comes here, so you won't get any help. Who paid you to kill me?"

"They will kill me if I tell you."

"That way you live a few days longer, because if you don't tell me, I'll kill you where you lie with pleasure."

"Help me."

"Just the way you helped me, bushwhacker."

Spur knew it was an obscene situation. He stood wearing nothing but a gunbelt, holding a .44 on an Indian lying in tall grass with four bullet holes in him already.

A gust of wind whipped a heavy pall of smoke over them and Spur ducked to avoid it. As he did Breed used his left hand, jerked a hideout from his ankle and pulled it up to fire at Spur.

The motion registered in Spur's side vision. He dove to the ground and fired the last round from his six-gun at the figure on the ground. There was no time to place his shot. The slug caught the Indian under the chin, smashed up through his mouth, through his brain and exited with a four inch square of scalp, hair and brain tissue.

Spur sat where he had stopped moving. Automatically he re-loaded his .44 from the rounds in the belt. There was no sense in checking on the Indian. He was as dead as any man ever gets.

Spur scowled as he went back for his clothes. He dressed quickly, put the picnic things in the big wicker basket and folded the blanket. He guessed that the horse and buggy might be a short way down the road.

He took one last look at the fire. It was all but out. It had died at the edge of the woods. He went to one spot and tramped out the last of the flames, then began his walk back to town.

He was wrong about the buggy. When he reached the main road, he ate a piece of chicken, finished the bottle of wine, and threw the blanket and the basket in the ditch.

Now he was sure. Katherine had set him up for a killing. She had picked the spot. She could have sent one of her men out in advance and had him all ready to blast Spur into a quick coffin. Katherine Sanford was also the counterfeiter. All he had to do was prove it.

CHAPTER FIFTEEN

Spur McCoy caught a ride with a farmer taking eggs and chickens into market. He got back to his hotel just after two o'clock. He moved to a new room again, resupplied his gun belt with rounds and carried some in his pocket. From now on he would move cautiously. If Katherine tried to have him killed in the country, she would undoubtedly continue the contract in town. He would use the back door and a low hat and change his habit patterns.

His prime job was to follow Katherine and hope that she led him to the next counterfeiting party. Nothing would happen there until dark. He changed jackets and slipped out the back door of the hotel through the kitchen, and went to see the banker, J. Anderson Dumbarton.

"We've found another twenty-five of the coins,"

Dumbarton said. "So far we are simply holding them, waiting the outcome of your investigation. How is it going?"

Spur told him he had a good idea. "Something may happen tonight, I'm not sure. If it turns out right, there should be enough funds to cover all of your counterfeit coins. That way you can simply replace the coins and we won't cause a panic in the public confidence of the double eagle."

"Good, this is one problem I'll be glad to have cleaned up."

"Have you ever thought about opening a branch of your bank in the Mexican Village?"

Dumbarton laughed. "No I haven't. I couldn't get in there in the first place."

"You might. With a partner. There are a lot of small merchants up there. They need a bank. You know who is doing the banking function now?"

"Juan Pico, and he's probably charging them twenty percent."

Spur smiled. "Mr. Dumbarton, I can see you've never met Juan Pico. He is tough, but he is also fair, honest and as far as I can tell, absolutely devoted to the betterment of his people. Do you know that right now he is holding more than three hundred double eagle counterfeit coins? Somebody flooded his merchants with them. If he wasn't holding them, it would wipe out every fifth store in the Village."

"He's holding over six thousand dollars worth? Amazing. We don't have a tenth of that amount." He rubbed his chin. "This Juan Pico, I've heard of him for years. Could you arrange a meeting with him?"

"Of course. I'm sure he would want to hand pick the people who worked in your branch. It would have to be bilingual all the way, and serve both anglos and Mexicans."

Dumbarton nodded. "Yes, we could work that out. And Pico, what would be his share?"

"You'll have to talk with him about that. But I would guess knowing his people had the services of a reliable bank would probably be reward enough for him."

"Maybe I've had this Pico all wrong."

"It's hard to know a man until you have met and talked with him for a while. Are you free now? Let's go and see Juan, and start discussions about this."

"Fine, but I'll leave my rings and watch and wallet here."

"Suit yourself, but you'll be safer in the Village than you are on any other San Francisco street."

The two men talked that afternoon and laid a foundation. The following day Juan Pico would visit Dumbarton in his office and they would make more plans.

Spur ordered a steak dinner sent to his room along with a pot of coffee and he ate every scrap of food. After that he had a short nap. Just before eleven o'clock he was up, dressed in black pants and a black shirt, ready for business. He had a feeling this was the night.

He planned to leave the hotel at midnight and drive straight to the Nelson Foundry. His plans changed when someone knocked on his door at

11:45. It was one of the men he had seen in Don Pico's office.

"Nelson's," the man said, still panting from running up the stairs. "We saw lights and heard voices and loud metal sounds. It began about twenty minutes ago."

Spur slipped on his gunbelt and buckled it, then put on a low crowned black hat.

"Thanks. This may be the time we catch them."

"Can we help you? Don Pico said we are at your command."

Backup. They could come in handy. The young Mexican touched a .44 on his hip. Spur nodded.

"Come on, we'll work it out as we ride."

Spur had changed his rented buggy for a rented saddle horse tied behind the hotel. They went out, again through the kitchen, and rode for the foundry. By then his plans were made. He left the two young Mexicans at the fence and told them that if he fired three shots in a row, they should come in, he would need help.

Like a dark shadow, Spur skimmed over the back fence, moved through the yard without a sound, then settled down behind some heavy sheet metal and watched. He saw the big Chinese man making a guard round of the fence. So they were here. When the way was clear, Spur moved toward the building where he could see a faint light. The heavy metal sounds had stopped about five minutes before, the Mexican lookout reported.

The Secret Service agent wasn't exactly sure what process they used, but he knew it couldn't be over yet. He moved up again, slid through a partially open dark door and was inside the building with the lights on. Three lanterns glowed at the far end. He worked his way slowly forward, making sure of each step.

After five minutes he could see two men moving around, then he spotted Katherine dressed again as a man. It looked as though they were in the plating process. Evidently they plated the round blank coins before they were struck off with the counterfeit dies. He moved closer. He could identify the man he had chased out from behind the gray house. He was helping a smaller man with the plating, dipping the coin blanks into a small vat that held the liquid gold. Spur had no idea how hot gold had to be to melt, but assumed that it had to be extremely hot.

He moved up again. The small man used a long handled, heavy metal dipper to move more molten gold from a furnace area to the vat where the blanks were immersed, shaken, and immersed again.

Spur had seen enough. With the dies in their possession this was plenty to convict.

He jumped out from his hiding spot and covered them with his six-gun.

"Hold it, right there!" he barked. "Nobody moves. You are all under arrest for counterfeiting." They froze from surprise more than fear. Spur walked forward. He had the three of them well covered. He could not see any guns but he was sure there were some around.

"Oh, shit!" Burke said.

The small man holding the cup sized dipper of

molten gold looked as if he was about to faint. He teetered on his feet, and the dipper wavered.

"Hold it steady!" Spur shouted. He was within six feet of them now. The youth he assumed to be Kate was furious but silent.

"Now, all of you lie down on the floor. Quickly! The small man with the molten gold looked at his treasure and shivered. He stumbled forward, tripped and the cup of pure gold jolted forward and splashed out of the container. Drops of it hit Spur's leg, bigger spots burned through his pants and into his ankle. Most of it splashed on the toe of his boot, the gold paltering the heavy leather in an instant.

As the gold burned into Spur he bit his lip and groaned at the searing pain. He concentrated on getting the gold off him and didn't notice Katherine slipping behind him swinging a half inch iron rod downward, striking his gun and slamming it out of his hand.

Burke pounced on Spur driving him to the floor and nailing his hands behind him.

"Now, big man, we get a good look at you," Burke said. "For as long as you live, that is. Good work, boss, you put him down just right."

"The gold! I spilled a whole ladle full of gold!" Tim Hackett cried.

"And a good thing you did," Katherine said. She had grabbed the six-gun and now held it on Spur. "Tim, get on with it, finish plating the blanks. We must hurry now. Even though I think Spur McCoy is working alone."

Spur lay on the floor. He could see two quarter

inch holes in his pants over his thigh where he had been burned. More serious was his ankle. The whole thing seemed still to be burning.

"So at last you know," Katherine said, looking down at Spur.

"I've known for several days, I just couldn't prove it. Now I can."

"You'll have a hard time proving it from the bottom of the bay. Because very soon you will be feeding the fishes."

"Want me to blow his brains out right now, Kate?" Burke asked. He had drawn his .44 and glared at Spur.

"Not here, we can't make any more noise than necessary. Maybe in time with one of the press strikes, that would cover up the sound nicely."

The plating was done and they walked Spur over to the lanterns lighting the huge press. Tim arranged the dies again, checked his set-up and then put one of the gold plated blanks in the die and tripped it. The powerful die press came slamming down on the blank, compressing the metal and leaving ridges and lines to form a near-perfect likeness of the double eagle. Tim examined the first one and smiled.

"Wonder how the great Spur McCoy would feel if his hand happened to get under that press?" Burke asked with a snarl. "Use his hand instead of a gold blank?"

Tim shivered, shaking his head. "Mess up the die, have to clean it off."

"What the hell, be worth it!" Burke yelped. "Hell,

I'll clean it up. Come on, this sonofabitch has it coming!"

Katherine smiled. "Why not, pain for pain I always say. Move over there, McCoy. Let's see how you stand pain." She sent Tim out to find Hop Choy and bring him in to help hold Spur. The big Chinese roared with anger when he saw Spur. When Tim told him what they were going to do he grinned. He put his hand over the die and gurgled what could have been a laugh.

Spur was hoisted up, his ankle still a roaring, almost debilitating agony. Burke pushed him beside the big press and Katherine and Hop Choy held him there. The big press was up. Hop Choy grabbed Spur's hand and pulled it over the lower die until it centered on McCoy's palm.

Spur shook his head. He knew what was happening, but the shock and the pain of the burn had him woozy. He shook his head again, saw his hand over the die where the gold blank should be. Slowly he realized what they were going to do. No, it wasn't right! No! He forced his mind to concentrate. He had to do something. The damn wires seemed to be down to his arm. He screeched at them in his mind. Move! Move!

Tim Hackett gritted his teeth as he reached with both hands, touching the safety handle with one, then tripping the press trigger with the other hand. Spur saw the press start to descend. It moved slowly, hundreds of pounds of pressure smashing downward.

He roared and the sound came out this time. It

wasn't only in his head. He saw Hop Choy jolt with surprise. At the same time Spur lunged backwards, dragging his hand out from under the die. Hop Choy didn't let go. He held fast to Spur's fingers. Hop Choy's hand and wrist moved over the die. Just as his wrist was over the lower die, the upper one powered down with tremendous force.

Hop Choy screamed, but it came out only as a terrified gurgle as the tongueless Chinese tried to jerk his hand away. He moved it only a fraction of an inch before the top die powered into his soft flesh and bone. In a second it was all over. Hop Choy's wrist was vomiting blood. His hand dangled by threads left where the die had cut out a round hold through his skin, tissue, and bones.

Hop Choy bellowed his shock and horror. He swung his hand at Spur but Spur and Burke had tumbled to the floor when Hop Choy released him. The nearly severed hand broke free and sailed onto the floor in front of Katherine. She stared down at it.

The huge Chinese bellowed in terror and agony, his voice in full volume. His bloody stump grazed Burke's shoulder, then came back and hit Burke in the face, slamming him sideways to the floor. He came up with his six-gun.

"Stop it, you wild, crazy Chink!" Burke screamed. He waved the gun at the marauding giant, who batted it aside and swung his good fist at Hackett, battering him away from the press, knocking him six feet down the shop to the floor.

Hop Choy kept on screaming, swinging at anything that moved. Spur edged into the shadows. He saw Burke moving away too. Then Burke stood, lifted the six-gun and fired.

The round went wide of Hop Choy, but he turned toward the sound.

Spur crouched in the shadows, working silently, deeper into the blackness. His ankle burned with a thousand demons but he tried to ignore it. He had to move or die, it was that simple. When Burke killed the crazed Chinese, he would come after Spur. McCoy made it to the door and rushed outside, putting all his weight on his left ankle for the first time. It gave way and he sprawled in the dirt.

In the shop behind Spur, Burke screamed at Hop Choy.

"Stop it, Choy! You're hurt damn bad. Let us help you. We can stop the goddamned bleeding and you'll live. You keep charging around this way and you won't, because you'll bleed to death in five minutes."

The huge Chinese neither heard nor understood. He could only see those who had pained him. He ran for the cowering Tim Hackett. Burke shot Hop Choy in the leg. He fell sideways, got up, but by then Hackett had vanished out of the pool of light coming from the three coal oil lamps.

The Chinese roared his anger and turned on Katherine still staring at the severed hand lying at her feet. Hop Choy walked toward her, his good right hand balled in a fist the size of a chopping block. He swung it back watching Katherine. She didn't move. Her eyes were glazed with fear.

Just as Hop Choy began to swing his big fist, Burke shot him in the forehead. The heavy slug penetrated his brain but still the mountain of a man came forward. Burke shot him again, this time the slug entered his right eye, slanted upward and cut off the brain's nerve centers to Hop Choy's legs. His knees buckled and he sat down, still staring at Katherine, then his eyes closed and he fell backwards.

Outside Spur had raised himself at the shots. He surged toward the back fence, hopping on his right foot.

The two Mexican lookouts saw him and one jumped over the fence to help. They lifted Spur over and were just turning when Burke ran up screaming at Spur. One of the lookouts fired a shot that grazed Burke's arm and drove him to cover. The three men beyond the fence scurried into deeper shadows, mounted up and rode for town.

It was nearly three in the morning when the Mexican doctor in the Village finished working over Spur. Don Pico stood by and asked only one question.

"Did you get the evidence you need?"

Spur shook his head. The doctor had used gas on him making everything fuzzy.

"I have enough on the two I guess are still alive. But the girl is a problem. I didn't see her there often enough to positively identify her out of her disguise. It could have been any woman about her size dressed that way. I have to be positive. I will tell Nelson about the problem and have him fire his night watchman and put on two new men until this is settled."

"Gold!" the doctor said holding up a tray with the splatters of gold he had removed from Spur's flesh and off the pants where it cooled before it burned through.

"It's yours," Spur said. "Gold is still worth $20.67 an ounce." He sat up wobbled a little and one of the men held him.

He looked at the bandage around his ankle. With a pair of pants on no one would notice. Now if he could walk. He pushed off the table to his feet and fell to the floor.

They helped him up and using a heavy cane he tried walking to the door. He walked back, then to the door and back again. After making the trip ten times, he dropped the cane and walked out to Olivera Street.

Spur thanked Don Pico for helping him.

"It is nothing, Mr. McCoy. Because of your help we are going to have a real bank here in the Village for the first time. It will make my people feel more like Americans, less like foreigners."

Spur nodded. "Good. I hope it works out. And I hope you insist that everyone learns to speak English. For your people to get out of poverty, they must know the language."

Don Pico sighed into the night air. "*Si*, that is true, but it is also harder. But I will soon start a school for adults. I will make it known that every adult must know English. Yes?"

Spur was taken in a carriage to his hotel and

helped up to his room. He rolled onto the bed and slept. He woke up at five in the morning, stood and walked around his room, then walked the length of the corridor three times. Good, his ankle was responding. The burns were not as deep as he had feared. He slept again, woke up at noon and walked again. After a quick lunch, he returned to the alley behind the gray house. He wore a large Mexican straw *sombrero* and a red and white *serape*, over his shoulders. The sun was not as hot today. He had brought his saddle horse, tied a few yards behind him.

The next move was up to Katherine.

CHAPTER SIXTEEN

Inside the gray house Spur McCoy watched from the alley, there was a heated discussion in progress. Three people had been talking for almost an hour.

"I say we go ahead and do the job like we planned," Burke said. "So we had some problems last night. We got the Chink dumped in the bay and got the place cleaned up so they won't notice anything. Way I figure it we're done with our coin making anyway. We might as well try for a big pay day."

Katherine Sanford had mixed feelings about it. She listened as Tim Hackett shook his head.

"Hey, we were lucky last night. That damn Chinaman could have killed us all. I say it's an omen, we do our money division right here, right now, and I can get out of here and vanish for a few years. We know practically for sure that this McCoy is a federal man. Who else would spend so much time on a counterfeit case? I say we call it quits right now, divide and disappear. McCoy will be down on us like a ton of horseshoes if we make another try at anything."

Katherine stood and walked the length of the room.

"The trouble is that both of you are right. We should stop and we should cap it with one big haul. There is supposed to be fifty thousand in gold coins in that bank. And it sits out there like a lonesome chicken surrounded by foxes. Then there is McCoy. He knows damn sure what's going on now. But why would he watch a bank?"

She studied the two men. Only two left out of the four. It would work better with five guns.

"You both agree that majority rules? Whichever way it goes the other one will dig in and help get the work done." The men nodded. "Then I say we take the bank this afternoon, right now, as soon as we can get out there. We have the saddle horses from the livery. Check your weapons and let's get out there."

Burke grinned. "I knew you would figure it out right. We go separately and meet at the bank."

"Yes, and don't be late. When we all get there we go right in. The safe will be open. No guards. Like taking candy from a baby."

Tim shrugged. "Hell, I figured I was done with all of this. I don't like guns."

"Well, bucko, you'll hold one today, and you'll use it if you have to," Burke said. "Hey, Tim, relax. I'm just trying to make you into a rich man."

Burke and Tim had left their horses in front of the house. They went outside and rode off. Spur missed them but he did see Katherine as she left the back door. He heard the screen slam and he faded behind a box in the alley, peeked out and watched her mount up and ride out at the far end of the alley. She was on a bay saddle horse. He would have no trouble following her.

She never looked behind. It was either a mark of confidence or stupidity, Spur wasn't sure which. She moved north, to the far edge of town and stopped half a block from a small cluster of neighborhood stores. Shortly two riders came up and joined her and the three talked for a minute, then rode separately down the street and tied up their mounts near the door to the small bank. Spur recognized Burke and the little metal expert from the foundry.

Bank robbery? Spur wondered. They were not depositing anything. That was certain. Spur rode forward and tied his horse to the rail, then edged up and looked inside the bank. All three had masks over their faces and their guns out. It *was* a robbery.

Spur checked the protective cover in the street. A horse trough sat directly across from the bank, forty feet to the front door. He ran there and lay behind it, waiting.

A woman moving down the boardwalk in front of the stores, stared at him in surprise, then hurried on.

Four minutes later the three in the bank came out. Spur put a round into the bank door over their heads.

"Drop your weapons, you're covered by ten guns. You don't have a chance."

Katherine pushed Tim toward the sound of the voice and sprinted for her horse. Spur fired once. Tim screamed and fell off the boardwalk into the dust of the street.

Burke and Katherine mounted up and rode hard. Spur couldn't shoot because a dozen people crowded around. He ran for his own horse, mounted and told someone to sit on the shot man and go for the police. Then he rode after them.

Following the pair was no problem. They rode fast and went nearly a mile before they split up. He followed Burke, the cowboy with the fast gun.

Spur had barely noticed the weather, but now he realized the sun was not shining, and the air smelled heavy and damp. The clouds boiled above them and before Spur had a chance to catch up to Burke, lightning split the skies apart, thunder rolled in and crashed, and rain came down like it was the forty day flood. It was a thunder shower trying to become a cloudburst. Spur wheeled his mount under a thick tree and waited out the rain.

When it tapered off to a fine mist, Spur went on a muddy street that angled back toward the downtown area. They were still out where great open spaces lay exposed. No buildings or even streets had been installed. Yet nowhere did he see the figure of Burke on his sorrel. The white mane and tail made it stand out like a flagpole.

Spur turned and galloped back to the bank. San Francisco police were there. They had hauled the small man back inside the bank where he had been identified and questioned. He grinned at them, steadfastly maintaining that he had done the whole thing himself.

When Spur arrived Tim changed his tune and demanded to be taken to jail at once. The bank had lost nearly three thousand dollars in gold coins. None was recovered from Tim Hackett's saddlebags.

Spur knew he should step forward, identify himself and take the city police into his confidence about the counterfeiting. He decided to tell them later, fearing that they would blunder and ruin his case against Katherine. He had seen it happen before, not here by the bay, but in other towns.

By the time he rode back to his hotel in the gentle mist, he was completely wet through and his ankle was burning as though it was inside a blast furnace. He put his horse behind the hotel at the rack and stumbled when he got off. He had to test his ankle three times and work at it before he could walk up the steps and into the side door. Then he hobbled to his second floor room and sprawled on the bed.

He knew that it was time to send word to the police, but he didn't. His ankle would be better soon and he would move in and close up Katherine and her little coin factory.

His forehead felt warm and he realized he had a fever. No! He could not get sick, he had a damn case to finish.

Katherine was furious when she returned to the

small gray house. She tied up her horse, carried the bank sack with the double eagles inside and pulled the six-gun from her holster. If she could only have had a shot at him! It was McCoy again. How could he possibly have known that they were there or that they were going to rob the bank? He must have seen them on the street and followed them. Clearly he knew about her disguise.

She paced the floor, then took the coins and opened the floor vault. From it she scooped a hundred of the counterfeits and placed ten genuine eagles on top of the pile in the heavy leather sack. It was time she began depositing some of the coins in banks around town.

At once she changed her mind. Too risky. Surely the San Francisco banks had been alerted to the counterfeits. She had to get away, south to Los Angeles! Yes, it was a long trip, but they would not be suspicious there. She had enough real coins to front the others.

Katherine took all the coins out of the impromptu floor safe and distributed them among several large leather bags. She could load them one at a time in her buggy. Quickly she changed into her afternoon dress, hid the sacks of coins in the closet and hurried home. She took only a few things in a carpetbag, some spare clothes, a letter of introduction from a banker, and then slipped out of the house without seeing her parents. She drove her best buggy to the alley and quickly loaded the leather pouches into it. She put some on the floor, others under the seat cushions. She was not dressed for the trip.

Back inside the house she changed into her boy's costume, put her hair up and packed her other clothes in her carpetbag.

She took one quick look around and ran out to the buggy. She had done it! She was a rich woman by her own hand. And she would go to Los Angeles, deposit the money, spend a few days and then return. She would write for letters of credit to the Los Angeles banks and have the money transferred to her bank up here. It would take a month, perhaps, but well worth it. The only stumbling blocks she could see were Spur McCoy and Foster Burke. She had expected Burke back before now. Hopefully McCoy had caught him before the rain hit and solved one of her problems.

Spur still felt light-headed as he turned his saddle mount into the far end of the alley behind the gray house where Katherine had changed her clothes. He blinked when he saw a fuzzy buggy and horse in back of the place. He shook his head to clear it and saw Katherine run out of the house carrying a carpet bag. She was in her young man disguise. Spur sat quietly as she stepped into the rig and drove out the other end of the alley.

McCoy had no idea where she was heading. But he knew he had to follow her. She could be on the way to her house on the hill. No, his fuzzy brain was not thinking straight. She never went up there in her disguise. Running away?

Possibly. What about Burke? She was probably running out on him too, taking his share of the gold. That sounded like Katherine Sanford. Spur kicked the mount into motion. He had to follow her, had to stay with her. His ankle churned with pain. His shoulder wound had started bleeding again, and his fever was a notch higher. He was in great shape!

After a half hour, Spur realized that they were heading out of town. It was the same road they had taken when they went to the picnic. This time there would be no picnic. The sky had cleared. It was not yet three in the afternoon.

He was as prepared as he was capable of under the circumstances. He had the six-gun and two boxes of rounds. He also wished he had his repeating Spencer. He didn't think he would need it in the civilized environs of San Francisco.

They passed the last businesses, and as they did Spur saw a sorrel with white mane and tail being ridden toward the buggy. It was Burke. It had to be. He rode alongside Katherine's rig and Spur wished he could hear the conversation:

He could imagine it: *Of course I'm not running out on you. I knew we had to get the gold away from the house. McCoy must have known where it was. It was get it away or lose it. You still get your half, Burke.*

How the talk actually went, evidently Kate won. She stopped the rig, and Burke tied his mount on behind and stepped into the buggy. Good, Spur had them both together. He felt sure the gold was on board too. Where was she heading? There were few little towns between San Francisco and Los Angeles, nearly four hundred miles to the south. Santa Barbara? There would be a bank there. Perhaps.

Spur shook his head and grabbed the saddle horn. He had almost toppled off his horse. He pushed his eyes open wide and stopped at the side of the street, which was quickly turning into a muddy country road. He would have to stay farther back now or they would notice he was following. He couldn't permit that. He had to wait until the proper time, when he would have an advantage, when he couldn't lose and they had no chance of winning. Spur shook his head to clear it. He prayed that the perfect time came soon. He wasn't sure how much longer he could sit in the saddle.

CHAPTER SEVENTEEN

Spur McCoy discovered that the route from San Francisco to Los Angeles in 1871 was not a grand highway. It was a poor imitation of a road and in places it came down to a track of a trail running across ranches and around bluffs and through the low mountain passes of the coast range. Never was it simple and easy.

Spur also found out that there were few inns along the way catering to the traveler, simply because there were few travelers. The stage did run, but it made its normal stops.

Spur figured he was about two hours behind the pair in the buggy when he came to the first stage coach overnight stop. These were usually spotted at twenty mile intervals. If a ranch was not available with its buildings and water supply, the coach company built a small station, crude, minimal and practical. Spur came to one of these down the coast about eighteen miles from San Francisco.

He looked it over carefully from the protection of some trees and made certain that Katherine and Burke had not stopped there. He wondered why they hadn't since it was after seven P.M. and the sun was almost drowning in the Pacific Ocean.

For the last mile Spur had been holding tightly to the saddle horn, not sure if he could sit the saddle or not. Once he had almost fallen off and the horse had stopped until he pulled himself upright. His head was pounding, his arm was bleeding again and his ankle felt like the liquid gold had just been splashed onto it.

When he rode up to the rail outside the coach stop, a wrangler saw him coming and hurried out and led the horse. He helped Spur down and walked him inside. Spur sat down at a long bench with a table in front of it and promptly lowered his head on his folded arms.

Someone brought him a steaming mug of coffee. The manager poured a slug of whiskey into the coffee and helped Spur drink it. Right then Spur could think of nothing better than a bottle of whiskey and a cot where he could sleep. They fed him first, then gave him a glass of whiskey and helped him to a bed. A woman came, put a new bandage on his shoulder. She chattered away about having done the same thing during the big war, but Spur barely heard her. She placed his foot in a pail of cold water and it stopped hurting for the first time since he was burned. Later she put some salve on the ankle and wrapped it. Spur McCoy knew nothing else until morning.

Five miles down the road, Burke and Katherine moved off the trail into a small bluff overlooking the ocean and camped.

She had brought along a few essentials when she left the house, including some blankets and two cooking pots. She knew she couldn't stay at the inns and coach stops with Spur looking for her. She also carried some food, and before they passed the last bit of San Francisco, Burke had stopped at a store and bought some bread, beans and bacon, the three B's of any travel cook, he told her.

Burke was an efficient camper. Within an hour after they stopped he had a cooking fire going, a spot cleared for their blankets, and a small lean-to built over the blankets. He made the lean-to of branches and some boughs from a pine tree.

"All the comforts of home," Katherine said after they had eaten and cleaned up the cooking things.

"Almost all the comforts," Burke said. He leaned in and kissed her lips. She didn't respond but neither did she pull away. She was thinking. All along she knew that she had not fooled Burke about not running out on him. She had been watching for a good moment to eliminate him, and she had the chilling idea that he would kill her at the first opportunity. Yes, the idea built. She could get him worn out with sex play and when he slept afterward she would shoot him. The idea was horrifying but there was no other way.

She returned his kiss, surprising him.

"There's no reason we can't be friends, Foss," she said softly, working a hand inside his shirt, rubbing his thick mat of chest hair, working down toward his crotch.

"I've always said we make a good team, Kate. I've got the know-how, and you have the contacts. We can take that town back there for plenty, then move on." He kissed her again, then put one hand over her right breast and rubbed softly.

"Foss, that feels so good! You know how to get me excited so quickly. Foss, why don't we seal our partnership right here by making love five or six times!"

"Yeah! Great idea. We will make a good team. You fuck so fine and you *like* it. A lot of women don't. Yeah, you and me, Kate, just you and me!"

She opened her shirt and pulled both his hands to her breasts. She knew she had him. He believed her about the partnership. So he wouldn't be trying to kill her. She could take her time, enjoy him once more for most of the night and it would be the last night Foss Burke ever knew.

She moaned in appreciation as he fondled her breasts.

"Damn, but you've got big tits, Kate, so big and beautiful, God! What a perfect set of tits!" He went down on them, kissing them and sucking them. She responded quickly and she didn't have to pretend. Any man could get her motor running, but she remembered the times with Spur and she knew he had touched her, and excited her more than any man ever had.

She pretended she was with Spur as Burke chewed on her breasts until she yelped with pleasure/pain. She pushed him away and stripped off the shirt. She wiggled out of the trousers and her cut-off drawers and sat on the blanket naked and passionate wanting to make love.

She helped him pull off his clothes, then turned on her back and put her legs high in the air.

"Right now, Foss darling, fuck me right now!"

Foss moved over her, not quite believing his good luck. All that gold and a good fucking woman like Kate! He kissed her flattened breasts and then probed and jammed and pushed into her with one hard stroke that brought a scream and then tears of joy from her as she yelled and shouted telling him he was the best man she'd ever had.

Foss had caught up with Katherine as she was riding out of town. He had gone to the gray house, saw that the gold was gone and wondered what she would do. He figured the banks wouldn't accept any counterfeits now, and the only thing she could do with them was to travel. For Kate that meant going south. He had gone down one street and missed her, doubled back and found her on the third main street out of town.

Now he was a little unsure. At first when he saw that she had gone he swore he would kill her. At the first chance he would fuck her and then kill her. But now with her new attitude, it might be different. He would go slow. He might give her a few days down the road. If he could get taken care of this well every night, goddamn, yes, he would give her a few more days.

Vaguely he realized that Katherine couldn't change her leopard's spots so quickly. Maybe she just wanted him to help her along the flight to Los Angeles.

Burke rammed her again and again, watching her smile and scream as she found her own climax four times before he was even ready. She was young. Hell she was rich too and she fucked. What more could a man want?

She locked her legs over his back and lifted her hips off the ground to meet his thrusts and within fifteen seconds he was blasting his load into her, grunting and yelping at the intensity of his climax.

Later they lay side by side on the blanket. The moon was out now and the clouds had all blown away.

"That was marvelous, Foss. Just wonderful. You're the best fuck I've ever had. The very best!"

"Kate, you're the most passionate woman I've fucked. You get so damned excited, you climax so quickly and you just keep going. I think this partnership is going to work in and out of bed."

"You bet it is, Foss. You bet! And we'll work at keeping it good. It won't go stale. Way I figure it is the way I told you. We take all the coins to Los Angeles and I'll use the letter of introduction from my banker, and we'll open an account in several banks. We'll put a bag of coins with some of our real ones on top. Let them check the top and they will be solid. We get it all deposited, then we go back to San Francisco, and we get the balances transferred up there. But the counterfeits stay in Los Angeles and they won't know where they came from."

"Fine, good thinking. We won't have to worry about robbing the stage coach anymore." He caught her breasts and rubbed them. She rolled over on top of him.

"Once more with me on top. I kind of like it up here. I can ride you like a pony, bucking and jumping and fucking away like crazy."

Foss laughed. "You are wild, a crazy, wild, best fucking woman in the world. Ride away, I'm ready." The idea of having to shoot the woman slid further and further from his mind as Foss reveled in the moment.

Katherine half lay and half sat on top of him, riding him like a pony, giving him satisfaction as well as enjoying it herself. A fleeting thought that she might need him down the road flashed through her mind, but she could find a guide at one of the coach stops if necessary. She could always put the gold in her big carpet bag and take the next stage south. This far from town it would be perfectly safe. Yes, it was sounding better all the time.

About two more fucks and Foss Burke would be so worn out he would sleep like a dead mule. *Planning, you have to plan all the time,* she told herself.

Later, she guessed it was a little after midnight, Katherine was still wide awake. Burke slept with one hand cupping her right breast. He snored softly, his naked form beside her on the blanket in the soft September night. She moved his hand. He mumbled but didn't awaken. His other hand cupped his genitals.

Kate eased away from him and crawled to the bottom of the blanket where they had left their clothes and their six-guns. She made sure his was there, took it and lay it in the buggy seat, then came back and checked the loads in her .32 caliber six-gun. All were there. She wondered how many she would need.

She had never killed anyone before. A sudden shiver of anticipation drilled through her. It was surprisingly like a climax! Her hand went to her crotch and stroked her clit twice and felt the sensations building. Yes, why not? A first! She kept stroking her clit and knelt across the blanket from him. He had been a good fuck, and now he would give her the ultimate sexual thrill—a death climax!

Her body responded faster. She pushed the magic node again and again. It came, that surging rapture, that ecstasy of boiling sexual triumph.

She aimed and pulled the trigger. The round missed Burke's heart, tore through a lung and severed several large arteries.

Her climax surged and she screamed in delight as Foss tried to sit up.

"Bastard!" he shouted. "Fucking, murderous bastard!"

Her climax built higher and she shot him again, then again and again. Each of the five times she shot Foster Burke her climax seemed to escalate into wild peaks of rapture. When the gun clicked on the empty round, she fell on the blanket so exhausted she couldn't move. For a half hour she lay there trying to recover.

Then she reloaded the little gun and worked herself up and did it all again, shooting him, climaxing, driving her passion into peaks of pleasure.

When the gun emptied and the last crashing climax left her, she lay down beside Burke's body and went to sleep.

Katherine was up early the next morning, flipped the blanket over Burke to avoid seeing him and put her gear in the buggy. She intended to drive to the next coach stop down the road, sell the buggy and horse and take the first coach south to Los Angeles.

So far her scheme was on schedule and progressing nicely. She presumed that she had eluded Spur McCoy or he would be on her trail by now. She smiled grimly. If he did find her, she would give him the same treatment that she had given Burke.

She shook her head in amazement. She still couldn't believe the fantastic heights to which she had risen when she worked her special magic on Burke.

Would it happen again? Could she make the same thrill occur with just any man? What about pulling the trigger when the man was inside her, fucking her?

Yes, there were new worlds to conquer. She would

make the experiment just as soon as she could. Perhaps at the coach stop if she had to wait over a night. She could even lure a stranger into the woods, experiment and be gone the next morning before anyone knew the man was missing.

And Spur McCoy. Yes! She almost hoped that he would find her. She would take triple pleasure in testing her new passion on him when his big cock was deep inside her!

CHAPTER EIGHTEEN

When Spur woke up the next morning, it was after eight. The morning stage had come in and driven on through to San Francisco. He sat up in his bed in the common room and saw that none of the other bunks was occupied. His head spun and whirled. He had to reach down to steady himself.

Better? Yes. He touched his forehead. The slight fever was gone. Even his ankle felt better this morning, but he wasn't going to enter any foot races.

His shoulder was stiff but at least it was not leaking blood. He was not sure about last night. He remembered that he ate some food and had some whiskey and the woman had fixed his shoulder. She made his ankle feel fetter.

Spur swung his feet to the floor and overcame the whirl of dizziness. Standing up was difficult, but once up he walked back and forth in the room until he was sure of himself. He adjusted his clothes, the old brown suit, and checked his six-gun. It was there and loaded.

The proprietor was surprised when Spur walked out to the main depot room a few minutes later.

"Thought you was out for a couple of days there, friend," the big man said as he eyed Spur.

"I'm feeling much better. What do I owe you for the night's lodging and nursing care?"

"Quarter should do it." He stopped. Curious. "You going to be moving on south? It's twenty miles on to the Gonzales Ranch."

"Heading that way. Did you see a buggy go past here yesterday? Pretty, long-haired woman and a man in it, trailing a sorrel with white mane?"

"Yep. Rode right on past. Figured they might stop for the night, but evident they were going to camp out."

"Thanks. I best get moving."

"Not before breakfast. Been saving some flapjacks and a pound of sausages for you. And coffee. Hate to see you leave in your condition. You a lawman?"

Spur didn't reply, just dug into the food when it appeared in front of him. The woman who brought it was short, round and happy. She smiled at him and he remembered her face from the night before. He still had the bandages around his ankle she put there.

"Before you try to sneak out of here, you let me look at that shot-up shoulder and your burned ankle. I'd be right down angry if you didn't let me play nurse one more time."

He nodded and she went back to the kitchen.

"Figured you had to be a lawman, otherwise any sensible man would be in bed getting himself well. But that ain't my row of corn to hoe. Just enjoy the victuals."

Spur ate until he could hold no more. There were four eggs on the side and a pitcher of maple syrup and a big cup of coffee the woman kept filling.

"Like to see a man eat," she said.

Spur thanked her. She checked his bandages and told him to get to a doctor for the shoulder as soon as he could.

"Course, I know you're heading away from the doctoring, but I got to tell you anyways."

The stable man had to help Spur mount his horse. He noticed that it had been brushed down, watered and given some oats to eat.

He gave the stable hand a silver dollar, paid the proprietor, and rode south down the trail.

There had been little traffic since the rainstorm. He saw the stage tracks and to one side the thin wheels of a buggy and one horse. Several times he lost them, the stage tracks were over them, which meant that the stage had traveled the road after the buggy had driven through.

Three more miles down the road, he saw the opposite was true. The buggy tracks were over the wide stage coach wheel marks. Which meant the buggy had been off the road for some time, probably all night, then moved out again in the morning. Spur was not far behind them.

The food and the kindly ministrations were all helping Spur to feel better. He brought the horse to a canter for a quarter of a mile, then eased her back. The jolting made him hurt all over. At least his head was clear.

He had to catch Katherine and bring her back for trial. He was sure she had the bank robbery gold and the counterfeit coins, otherwise Burke would not have gone with her. He could look forward to a double job as soon as he caught them.

Every half hour he put the horse in a trot and kept at it for as long as he could stand the jolting. He hoped he was gaining on them.

Just before noon the trail wound around a hill and came out near the coast where it crossed a small stream. A flash flood had washed out the temporary bridge made of logs and laid end ways in the stream. The water was not more than a foot deep now. Ahead he could see that a buggy had tried to cross it. The stage coach probably crossed as well, but the fording was not as kind to the narrow wheels of the buggy. The rear wheels were sunk in the mud up to the axle.

Spur turned into the trees and watched the rig. For ten minutes nothing moved. Then he saw a small figure get out of the buggy and step gingerly into the water. There was no mistaking the carriage or the stance. It was Katherine. Where was Burke? Spur noticed that the sorrel was no longer tied to the back of the carriage. Had Burke gone ahead for help?

No, help was closer to the rear. The second horse

would have been enough to pull the buggy out of the mud. Spur had a chilling thought. Burke was not helping get the buggy out because he was no longer with Katherine. Spur guessed the fast gun had met a faster gun and was probably at the overnight camp the couple must have made.

He rode through the woods, circling around so he could come up to the buggy in the cover and not be seen. Brush and live oak came to within twenty yards of the stalled rig.

Spur McCoy left his horse tied to a tree and went the last twenty yards on foot. When he looked around the oak tree closest to the buggy, he saw Katherine Sanford facing the buggy and screaming at the horse. She tugged at the bridle urging the horse forward, but the horse could not pull it out. She raged and swore at the horse. Finally she took out her pistol and aimed at the animal's head and fired. At the last moment she had lifted her aim over the head to miss. The horse shied away as far as the traces would let it and lunged forward, but still the rig was mired.

She shoved the gun back in the holster and began to unhitch the animal from the buggy. It was immediately obvious that she did not know what she was doing.

Spur stopped her with a pistol shot over her head.

"Morning, Katherine Sanford. Don't move, that first shot was a warning. The next will cut your pretty little legs right out from under you."

She glared his way.

"Don't just stand there, stupid. Come help me get

this rig out of the mud."

"First, some talk. One: You are now under arrest for counterfeiting U.S. gold coins. Two: You are under arrest for bank robbery. Three: You are under arrest for the murder of an accomplice in said bank robbery, one Foster Burke. Four: You are now to take the six-gun from your holster and drop it in the stream, then lace your hands on top of your head. Do you understand all these directions?"

She drew the gun slowly, then fired the last four shots in the direction of his voice. She didn't move. When the gun was dry she tossed it in the creek, and put her hands on her head.

"It's safe to come out now, Spur McCoy, you big bad United States Government agent."

Spur walked out, his gun back in the holster.

"I should have shot you when I had the chance," she said.

"The same way you shot Foster Burke?"

"No, not that way, something different, more interesting."

Spur came up and stood in front of her.

"I'm going to check to see if you have any other weapons. Don't move or I'll knock you down." Spur patted her down along shapely legs, around her waist, up to her breasts. She had no other weapons.

"Now what?" she asked.

"Now we get you unstuck and we drive back to the San Francisco police who take you into custody on three charges."

"Nobody will believe it."

"All we need are twelve good and true men to

believe it, and you'll be in prison for the rest of your life."

"It's a long way back to San Francisco."

"Will you stay here while I go get my horse, or do I have to tie you up?"

She glared at him, then noticed his limp.

"That foot Tim splashed with molten gold hurt you a little? And I see your shoulder is still bleeding. Too bad. I'll stay. It's a lot of miles to San Francisco."

Spur brought up his horse, tied it to the frame of the buggy, and with one surge the two horses pulled the rig up to dry land.

Spur got on his horse and they towed the buggy back across the ford with no trouble. He made Katherine walk across in her boots and pants, then told her to sit down on the grass while he inspected the buggy.

He found the gold, and a .44 six-gun.

"Burke's?" Spur asked.

"It was. He gave it to me."

Spur found nothing else dangerous on board, so let her get in and tied his mount to the rear. Spur took the reins.

A half hour later she spoke for the first time.

"You better stop, I have to go to the bathroom."

Spur looked at her with suspicion, shrugged and stopped the rig. He went with her to the side of the road where she let down her pants and squatted.

"You could hold my hand and squeeze," she said.

"You won't get any hand holding in prison."

He heard his horse snort and looked at the rig,

and when he glanced back she stood up, kicked off the pants and was unbuttoning her shirt.

"That won't work, Katherine. I'll take you right through to San Francisco naked as a new born if you want it that way."

She threw the shirt down and ran to him, pushing her body against his and talking fast.

"Spur, once more! Think how long it's going to be until I have a man again. Come on, Spur, fuck me just once more here in the open while I'm still free. Just one more good one!"

Spur pushed her down and she fell on the grass at his feet.

"Is that how you caught Burke off guard, with his pants off, maybe even inside you?"

"Burke was going to kill me, I just beat him to it."

"It won't work here, forget it. Do you want to dress again, or ride on into town that way?"

Before she could answer a rifle spoke nearby and the lead whistled past so close to Spur's nose that he could smell the heat. He dropped down, but had nothing to hide behind.

The voice that came from the brush was southern-mean. Spur reached for his six-gun.

"Your hand touches that iron, you get a .50 caliber slug right in your belly. You want that, friend?"

Spur moved his hand away from his gun.

"Now that's good. You, pretty baby, stand up and turn around slow, want to get me a good look at all them tits and cunt."

"Well, sure. This guy was attacking me. You

came just in time. I can be nice to you, would you like that? Right here, right now!"

She turned around twice, then stood watching the woods.

A man emerged with his rifle covering them. Spur frowned, rawhiders, and there would be more than one. Probably renegades left over from the war, living off the land, robbing and killing anyone they ran across, living in the hills and woods, moving all the time. To them human life was no more important than that of a rabbit, a dog or a mosquito.

The man was thin and tall, clad in dirty jeans and a ragged shirt too large for him. His beard was greasy, his hair matted under a filthy black hat. Small dark eyes showed from a smoke and dirt stained face. His fingernails were dirty and ragged, his teeth half black stumps.

He turned Katherine around again, then rubbed her breasts.

"Damn good tits, little whore." He turned and called toward the buggy.

"Come on in, Sacks, I got'm by the tits." He laughed and kicked Spur in the leg. "You got any cash money, boy?"

"Yes."

"Get it out, slow. And lay that six-gun over there on the grass."

Spur did, putting his wallet beside it. He looked up to see a small woman dressed in the same kind of ragged clothes, just as filthy as the man.

"Leave her tits alone, you bastard!" the woman

shrilled.

"Lilly Mae, ain't them something. Look at all them tits! Christ, she got twenty times the knockers you got."

"Shut up, stupid. She'd sooner shoot you as fuck you. Now you gonna do it, or should I?" Spur saw that she carried a sawed-off shotgun. The barrel was not over eight inches long.

"Now wait a minute," the man argued. "She offered, Lilly Mae, before I said a dang thing. She offered!"

"That's right," Katherine said. "I'll go down on you right now, you open your jeans. And I'll fuck you twice a day. You'll have these good tits all to yourself. Shoot the old hag there and take me with you. Shoot both of them!"

The rawhider grinned at his woman. "Damn, Lilly Mae, she's like us. God, what I'd give to fuck her just once. Lilly Mae, you put down the shotgun and look through the buggy. You come back and it'll all be over, then we finish our business and move on. Remember that redhead last week? He was your turn. This one is my turn, then it'll be even again."

"Shit, what a bastard you are," Lilly Mae said. She shrugged and lay down the shotgun. "Hell, make it fast, I don't like being this close to no highway." She walked back toward the trail.

At once the man opened his pants and his hard penis shot out. Katherine hesitated only a fraction of a second, then she opened her mouth and knelt in front of him and went down. The man moaned in delight, the rifle lowering. Spur eyed his six-gun forgotten three feet from him. The shotgun was ten feet away. But his own pistol was a chance.

Spur lay where he was, watching the rawhider. He was getting excited. Suddenly the rawhider pushed her away.

"Get on your hands and knees," he said. He leered at Spur, and laughed. "Damn, dog fashion fuck!"

Katherine went to her hands and knees quickly. She was sideways to Spur now. The man still held the rifle in his right hand near Spur as he knelt behind Katherine trying to make the right connection. When he was inside he yelped with delight and howled like a dog, his head high, his eyes closed.

Spur dove toward the gun, rolled in the grass on his shot-up shoulder, caught up the weapon and fired three times. The first round missed, the second took a half inch off the rawhider's nose, and the third went in just behind his ear, roared through his brain and came out over his eyes. The force of the slug knocked him to the left away from Katherine who dropped to the grass on her stomach.

A scream of fury sounded near the buggy, then Lilly Mae came running toward them firing a six-gun.

"No, no, not me!" Katherine shouted. "I want to go with you. He killed your man, Spur shot him!" Katherine sat up as she said it. Lilly Mae was twenty yards away, and Spur had held his fire. He still had two rounds and couldn't waste them. He looked at the shotgun, still six feet away. It was double barreled.

Lilly Mae screamed again and ran toward them,

firing again. Now Spur saw she had two six-guns. Spur fired a warning shot, then she fired twice more.

One of the rounds caught Katherine in the chest, staggering her. She slumped to the left. Now she was waving her hands, pointing to Spur. Lilly Mae shot twice more and both rounds caught Katherine Sanford in the face, one tearing upward into her brain, destroying vital nerve centers and slamming her backward into the long sleep of death.

Spur fired his last round at Lilly Mae, missed and rolled toward the shotgun. He came up with it as the woman was frantically reloading one of the six-guns.

"Put it down, Lilly Mae," Spur said. "Drop it now."

"Fucking shotgun ain't loaded," she screamed.

Spur snapped in the last round and brought up the gun.

Spur fired. The buckshot caught her in the stomach and almost tore her in half. She jolted backwards and screamed a last threat but gurgles of blood were all that came out.

Spur ran back to Katherine. She was dead the moment the bullet struck. The other two were gone as well. He had no shovel. He picked up Katherine and took her back to the buggy. There he dressed her in her pants and shirt and sat her in the seat. Then he collected the shotgun and two handguns and the rifle, and drove slowly back to the stage coach inn where he had spent the previous night.

They would be surprised to see him. He would hire one of the men to come back and bury the two. Katherine he would take on into town. He should be able to get there well before midnight. There would be a lot of explaining to do, and he would have to identify himself again. He looked at Katherine and shook his head. For a girl with all the advantages, she had taken the wrong road. She had been willing to go with the rawhiders, to kill the other woman and become the man's new woman, to become a rawhider herself, just so she could stay out of jail.

Spur urged the horse on faster. He had a corpse, and what he guessed was about sixty thousand dollars in counterfeit gold double eagles.

He had to deliver them tonight.

CHAPTER NINETEEN

Spur tied up the horse in front of the San Francisco police station just before 10 P.M. and called a passing officer to bring out the captain in charge.

"I've got a dead body here I want to talk to him about," Spur said and the man ran inside quickly.

Spur wasn't sure how long he could stand on his ankle. It was throbbing again. The watch captain came out quickly, his name was Streib. Three officers stood behind him.

"Is this a joke, sir. You have a corpse out here?"

Spur motioned at the figure in the buggy and the captain investigated quickly.

"Call the undertaker or the mortician or whoever handles that sort of thing. Then notify her father. The lady is Katherine Sanford, daughter of Amos Sanford."

"You're joking," Captain Streib said.

"I'm not joking. My name is Spur McCoy and I am a United States Service agent. I'll show you my credentials later. Right now there is forty or fifty thousand dollars worth of gold double eagles on this buggy. I want some lock boxes I can transfer it to until I can go over it and separate the real ones from the counterfeit."

"You must be drunk!"

"Captain Streib, am I going to have to call your police chief from his home? Just do what I ask you. Katherine Sanford is the counterfeiter. She also robbed the Thirtieth Street bank yesterday. Now bring out those lock boxes and send someone to take the body."

It was a half hour before the undertaker came. Amos Sanford stormed up at about the same time. He was a short man, slender and wiry. He carried a silver headed walking cane he liked to wave around. He stood in front of Spur as the undertaker's buggy rolled away. Tears showed in his eyes.

"Sir! I demand some explanation! How did my daughter die? Did you shoot her? Why did it happen?"

Spur quietly told him the story, what she had been doing, and how the rawhiders killed her.

"I don't believe any of it!" Amos Sanford said through clenched teeth. "I'll have you charged with murder before daylight. I have some powers in this town. The chief of police is a good friend of mine."

Spur's kind attitude changed. "Good, because

when it comes out in the papers what Katherine did, the people she killed and had killed, the counterfeiting and the bank robbery, you are going to need all the friends you have. Besides, the Secret Service functions directly for the President of the United States, and *he* happens to be a good friend of mine."

Spur walked over to the buggy and supervised the loading of the gold coins in the two lock boxes. He searched the rig three times, and when he was certain all the coins were in them, he snapped the padlocks on the hasps and took the keys.

It was almost midnight.

Spur went inside the station, saw that two locked boxes were placed in the police safe and the door shut, then he turned to Captain Streib. He took the thin card from between two others in his wallet and showed it to the policeman.

"If you need further proof, send a wire to William Wood, Director, the Secret Service, Washington, D.C. He will confirm my authority and description."

Captain Streib read the card and handed it back.

"No, Mr. McCoy, that won't be required. You just gave me a start hauling a corpse right up to my door, and a buggy with fifty thousand dollars in it."

"Sorry, it just turned out that way. Do you have a doctor on call? I have a bad ankle that needs attention."

A half hour later Spur sat in a small medical office two blocks from the police station. A bear of a man worked over the ankle, shaking his head.

"Infection. I just hope we can stop it in time so you don't lose the foot. Looks bad." He applied some medication and told Spur to stay off the foot for a week at least.

"The shoulder is healing. Would do better if you stop breaking it open. May bleed a little more, but it's coming along well. You tend to get yourself hurt a lot, don't you, Mr. McCoy."

"Seems as how, Doc."

Spur found a police rig waiting for him outside the doctor's office to take him to his hotel. He fell into bed and slept at once.

At 8 A.M. the next morning a knock on his door awakened Spur. There were two reporters from the newspapers. He told them to come back in two hours.

His ankle was swelled half again its size. He sent notes to J. Anderson Dumbarton and Juan Pico, explaining his injury and asking if they could meet him in his room at eleven o'clock. Then he went back to sleep.

Spur was up and wearing a clean shirt and his foot rested on a pillow when the two men arrived.

"We heard the news," Dumbarton said, a big grin on his face. "Amazing. It was that pretty little Katherine Sanford behind the whole thing. Remarkable."

Juan Pico smiled. "And this should stop the flood of counterfeit coins, right?"

Spur told them what had happened. "We should have most of the counterfeits. In cases like this there are always a few floating around that haven't been found yet. What I suggest is that Mr. Dumbarton wait a reasonable time and then talk to Amos Sanford. Tally up all the losses on the counterfeits by everyone, you, Don Pico, other banks, and build in a contingency for those not found. Show Sanford the figure. He may simply write a check for the amount. If not you might suggest that the cash come from Miss Sanford's property. She owns that gray house we mentioned. If this doesn't work, you may have to threaten a civil suit to recover damages, but I don't think Mr. Sanford would let it go that far."

Don Pico, nodded. "This all seems fair and proper, Mr. McCoy. My people thank you. More than two dozen small shop owners thank you for saving their stores. To show our appreciation we are holding a *fiesta* tonight in Olivera Street. Everyone is invited. There will be music and dancing and more food than anyone can eat.

"Mr. Dumbarton has promised to come. We are making good progress on talks about the new Olivera Street Bank."

Dumbarton agreed. He looked around the room. "I've made some other arrangements. There will be a nurse coming in at noon with your lunch. She will be on duty here twenty-four hours a day until you can get around. The doctor said to stay off the foot, right? She'll be in the room next door, but we'll have a hole cut in the wall and a string put through so you can ring a bell whenever you want her."

"There's no need for that . . ." Spur began. Both men looked at him sternly. "All right, thank you," he said meekly.

"There will be a buggy at the door for you and your nurse at six tonight, so you can come to the fiesta," Don Pico said.

The men started for the door. Dumbarton turned.

"McCoy, just relax, rest and get well. We might need you again out here. We want you to think well of San Francisco."

As they went out a bell boy came in with two telegrams. One was from General Halleck, his immediate superior in Washington. It read:

"Good work re counterfeiting stop Hurry and get well stop have two more assignments waiting stop Halleck."

"Figures," Spur mumbled, moving his foot on the cushion. And knowing Halleck his next job probably would be somewhere in the Texas desert or the wilds of Montana.

The second wire was from Fleurette Leon, his assistant in the St. Louis office, and cute as a fluffy kitten. He read the message:

"Hear you've done it again stop Go easy on that hurt ankle stop Please don't get shot anymore stop We need you stop Hurry home stop All my love stop Fluerette."

Spur put down the wires and smiled. It was nice to be appreciated by someone, even if she was a slip of a girl half a continent away.

The knock on the door came softly. He called for the person to come in.

Spur McCoy stared. She was tall and slender, with wheat straw colored hair billowing around her face and shoulders. Soft blue eyes twinkled at him over a pug nose and dimples dented her cheeks. She was so pretty, and her smile so radiant that he kept staring.

She laughed softly, and the animation in her face was delightful.

"Mr. McCoy?"

"Ah . . . yes. Yes."

"Oh, good, at first I thought I had the wrong room. I have your lunch. I'm your nurse."

Spur shook his head. "Tell me I'm not asleep and dreaming. This must be a dream. You are absolutely gorgeous! You're the most beautiful woman I've ever seen."

She smiled and he knew she had heard compliments before.

"Well, aren't you nice! But remember, the doctor said you were not to get excited or walk around. Our job is to get you well."

"I may stay sick for six months," Spur said and she laughed softly.

"They said you were a perfect gentleman. Are you really from New York, and Washington, D.C.? Have you really met President Grant?" Her soft blue eyes were wide with wonder.

"Yes, to all three. I just remembered. I didn't have any breakfast. Did you really bring me lunch?"

"Oh, gracious! I almost forgot." She went into the hall and rolled in a small cart with a covered tray on it. She closed the door, then looked at him quickly.

"Is it all right to close it?"

"Fine with me. After all, you're the nurse."

"I wanted to ask." She uncovered the tray, showing him two kinds of sandwiches, a bowl of ranch stew, two desserts, a glass of milk and a pot of coffee.

"We want to be sure you eat to keep up your strength."

"I'll try. You have to eat with me."

"Oh!" She shrugged. "All right."

He ate and she nibbled on a sandwich. He caught the scent of her long blonde hair as it came close to him. She wore a blue dress that swept the floor and buttoned to her neck. It was molded to her body and showed good breasts and a small waist.

When the lunch was over, she cleared the tray and rolled it outside the door, then came back. She adjusted the pillows around his head and his foot and checked the bandages.

"Your foot is fine. The doctor will come tomorrow to check it. You are a most important man in town. Mr. Dumbarton says we have to take care of you in every way. Now, let's look at your shoulder. Off with the shirt." She unbuttoned it for him, and helped him out of it.

When her fingers touched his shoulder to check the bandages he felt a tingle. The cloth showed no bloodstains.

"There, that is fine, too." She stood and smiled. "Now I think you should have a nap."

"I should get at least one kiss good night," Spur said.

She sat on the bed beside him.

"That's not usual nursing procedure."

"But you are not the usual nurse. You are a beautiful, wonderful, marvelous, highly desirable nurse."

"Oh, thank you! And you are as nice as they said. Maybe just one small goodnight kiss."

She leaned down and kissed his cheek, but lingered. He took her face in his hands and brought her lips to his. She didn't protest. Spur kissed her tenderly, then with more force, and brushed her lips with his tongue.

She leaned away and he gave up her lips. She didn't move far.

"Now, that was nice, Mr. McCoy. But, gracious, you aren't asleep yet. Do you need one more?" He nodded. She bent down to him gently, then touched his hair with her hand and this time her tongue brushed his lips. He opened them, then his tongue darted through into her mouth. The game began of search and find, touch and retreat and her tongue played along.

She pulled away gently. "I don't think you're going to sleep."

"I could sleep much better if the door were locked and the key turned half around in the lock," Spur said.

She grinned, kissed him gently and stood. "Mr. McCoy that was not in any of the nursing training I took. However, I think it might be good therapy."

"I don't know your name," Spur said.

She locked the door as he asked, then came back. "I'm Millicent, Millicent Young. Call me Milli." She sat on the bed beside him.

"Now for that therapy," Spur said. She bent down and kissed his nose, then his cheeks, and then his mouth. Her lips came to his softly and parted. She moaned in delight as his tongue penetrated her mouth. She stretched down until she was lying beside him, half on top of his good side. She purred.

When the long kiss ended she sat up and unbuttoned three of the fasteners down the front of her dress.

"It's warm in here," she said.

Spur agreed and motioned for her to bend lower. He finished undoing the buttons to her waist. She bent down and he worked his hand under the chemise and captured one of her hanging breasts.

"Oh, dear!" she said, gasping slightly. "That is so, so delightful!"

Spur sat up beside her, pushed the dress off her shoulders and spread kisses across her chest above the white chemise. Then he pushed the chemise straps down and moved it lower until one pink-tipped breast showed.

"You really shouldn't," she said softly.

"I know," Spur said and bent and kissed the breast. Milli sighed softly. He licked the throbbing breast and watched her nipple enlarge and stiffen. A moment later he worked on her other breast. He found her hand and moved it down to his crotch and helped her unfasten the buttons on his fly.

"Milli, I think this is going to be a slow but fantastically successful recuperation. I'm going to need a week at least to get well enough to travel, maybe two weeks."

"Spur McCoy, I'll certainly do everything possible to make your recovery just as pleasant and memorable as I can."

"I was hoping you would," Spur said and kissed her pulsating breast again.